# DESPERATE
# DETROIT
And Stories of Other Dire Places

# DESPERATE DETROIT

## DETROIT

And Stories of Other Dire Places

# LOREN D. ESTLEMAN

TYRUS
BOOKS

Published by
TYRUS BOOKS
an imprint of F+W Media, Inc.
10151 Carver Road, Suite 200
Blue Ash, OH 45242. U.S.A.
www.tyrusbooks.com

Hardcover ISBN 10: 1-4405-9620-4
Hardcover ISBN 13: 978-1-4405-9620-9
Paperback ISBN 10: 1-4405-9623-9
Paperback ISBN 13: 978-1-4405-9623-0
eISBN 10: 1-4405-9621-2
eISBN 13: 978-1-4405-9621-6

Printed in the United States of America.

10  9  8  7  6  5  4  3  2  1

"The Black Spot" previously published in *Ellery Queen's Mystery Magazine*, March/April 2015. "The Tree on Execution Hill" previously published in *Alfred Hitchcock's Mystery Magazine*, August 1977. "Sincerely, Mr. Hyde" previously published in *Alfred Hitchcock's Mystery Magazine*, July/August 2014. "You Owe Me" previously published in *Ellery Queen's Mystery Magazine*, September/October 2015. "A Web of Books" previously published in *Alfred Hitchcock's Mystery Magazine*, February 1983. "State of Grace" previously published in *An Eye for Justice* edited by Robert Randisi, copyright © 1988 by Mysterious Press, ISBN 10: 0892962585, ISBN 13: 9780892962587. "The Used" previously published in *Alfred Hitchcock's Mystery Magazine*, June 1982. "Bad Blood" previously published in *Alfred Hitchcock's Mystery Magazine*, July 1986. "Cabana" previously published in *The Armchair Detective*, Spring 1990. "Lock, Stock, and Casket" previously published in *Pulpsmith*, Summer 1982. "Diminished Capacity" previously published in *Alfred Hitchcock's Mystery Magazine*, December 1982. "Saturday Night at the Mikado Massage" previously published in *Alfred Hitchcock's Mystery Magazine*, November 1996. "How's My Driving?" previously published in *Alfred Hitchcock's Mystery Magazine*, January/February 2008. "The Pioneer Strain" previously published in *Alfred Hitchcock's Mystery Magazine*, October 1977. "Flash" previously published in *Murder on the Ropes* edited by Otto Penzler, copyright © 2001 by New Millennium Entertainment, ISBN 10: 1893224333, ISBN 13: 9781893224339. "Evil Grows" previously published in *Mystery: The Best of 2001* edited by Jon L. Breen, copyright © 2002 by I Books, ISBN 10: 0743445015, ISBN 13: 9780743445016. "The Bog" previously published in *Wild Crimes: Stories of Mystery in the Wild* edited by Dana Stabenow, copyright © 2004 by Signet, ISBN 10: 045121286X, ISBN 13: 9780451212863. "Now We Are Seven" previously published in *Ghost Towns* edited by Martin H. Greenberg and Russell Davis, copyright © 2010 by Pinnacle, ISBN 10: 0786019565, ISBN 13: 9780786019564.

Cover design by Frank Rivera.
Cover image © Andrey Bayda/123RF.

*This book is available at quantity discounts for bulk purchases.*
*For information, please call 1-800-289-0963.*

# Contents

# Preface

## The Desperate Business of Crime

It's struck me, in the course of writing about it, that crime is the most durable small business we have.

The rule of supply and demand applies to illegitimate enterprise just as it does to legal commerce, albeit without interference from government regulations and lip service about Giving Back; the characters in these stories never gave back anything, because they put their lives on the line acquiring it. No one can adequately explain algebra, the butterfly effect, or why Frankie Valli and the Four Seasons sounded so much like a loose fan belt, but everyone can grasp the significance of a suitcase full of cash. Nowhere else is desperation more obvious to the eye and touch.

Alfred Hitchcock once explained the difference between mystery and suspense in the context of a stage play: When the cast is aware that a bomb is about to go off and the audience isn't, it's a mystery. When the audience is aware that a bomb is about to go off and the cast isn't, it's suspense.

For going on four decades I've written stories about desperate men and women trying to find their way back to the lives they'd sought to escape from in the beginning; Dorothies groping their way along the Yellow Brick Road back to the bleak Kansas they'd hoped to leave behind. That formula doesn't apply to all the protagonists in the stories that follow, but at the core, all are underdogs: cold-blooded killers who are somehow better than their victims, juvenile delinquents denied a second chance when it counted, clerks caught in the middle, psychotic killers who knew no alternative, survivors in a foreign world, losers who long to be winners, ordinary people with dark secrets, fanatics drawn into darkness by their fixations, someone putting his life on the line for something of greater value to himself than the world knows; people you read about every day in the papers, see on TV, glimpse on the Net (and sometimes in the mirror). Every one of them is a star in his own movie, if the world would just see it.

It would be difficult to select a place to which the term "desperate" applies more appropriately than Detroit.

I was fourteen years old when I tuned in to a local TV station and saw military tanks trundling four abreast up Woodward Avenue, the city's main street. This was at the height (or depth) of the war in Vietnam, and footage of that tragically unnecessary conflict aired daily; I thought this was what I was witnessing, until I recognized the Fisher Building towering in the distance.

Suddenly, guerrilla warfare had come to my own backyard.

This is what happened: In July 1967, a routine police raid on a "blind pig" (regional parlance for an illegal after-hours drinking and gambling establishment) went very wrong very fast as a mob of residents fell upon the team of officers with rocks and bricks. Decades of unrest fostered by a predominately black population policed and governed by a predominately white establishment burst into rage. By the time the National Guard and then the U.S. military managed to quell the disturbance, 3,800 people had been arrested, 1,700 stores had been looted, 1,383 buildings burned, 347 people were injured, and 43 people had been killed. This led to a sharp hike in the crime statistics, peaking in 1974 with 801 murders. In that year, Coleman A. Young took office as the city's first black mayor, but after twenty years of his administration Detroit's image had not improved. It was referred to by the press as Dodge City, and when it was pointed out that the West's wildest cowtown paled in comparison to the Motor City's plight, "Murder City" took its place.

Today, the situation has improved considerably, with various civic improvements ongoing and major businesses moving in and brightening the employment picture, but unscrupulous opportunists like former mayor Kwame Kilpatrick, currently serving a decades-long sentence in federal prison for corruption and racketeering, periodically underscore Detroit's lingering reputation as a desperate place.

All this is useful to a crime writer, offering no end of inspiration, but as someone whose global outlook has always come filtered through the metropolis to the east, I continue to root for its renaissance. I like the place. Whine though its leaders and media personalities will about the cheap shots taken by outsiders, the residents of the neighborhoods are too busy paying bills and trying to improve their lot to behave like petulant children. They make the best of what they have, in the conviction, however faint, that things can only get better; and they take steps to see that they do.

It's unlikely that Detroit will ever be what it was in the 1920s and late 1940s, when it was expected to take its place as the fourth most populous city in the nation. There are too many variables, and its status as a great manufacturing center is ill-equipped to challenge the rapid-fire progress of technology. But I hold faith in its basic strength of character. From its founding to the present, its history has been a history of violence, but it has also been a history of hope.

The culprits in the stories that follow, whether they ply their dark trade in Detroit or other places similarly suited to their methods, believe that in desperate times the very structure of civilization has collapsed and nothing is forbidden. As J.R. Ewing put it on *Dallas*, "Once you set aside integrity, the rest is easy." Similarly, once you choose the forbidden path, assault and homicide are no longer off the table.

Crime is free enterprise in the purest definition of the term. It's pass/fail, with reward to the first and punishment to the second. And any place is desperate where desperate people congregate.

*—Loren D. Estleman, November 2015*

# The Black Spot

*Just when it seems I've gotten all I can out of Peter Macklin before he devolves into one of those tiresome series characters who exist only to run up a body count, he surprises me with an exhilarating domestic situation. "The Black Spot" brings him full circle back to where he began: doing what he does best despite the distractions of home. Even cold-blooded killers worry about paying their bills.*

They said Leo Dorfman had forgotten more about the law than most lawyers ever knew.

A couple of his clients, currently serving as guests of the federal government, agreed.

He'd been eighty for as long as Peter Macklin could remember, a stopped clock now in semiretirement, working out of his Redford Township dining room in one of the three-piece suits he continued to wear every day. Mrs. Dorfman, brown and wrinkled in a woven sun hat, sleeveless blouse, and yellow shorts, knelt in her flower garden outside. Macklin glanced at her from his seat opposite the lawyer's at the round table.

"Don't worry about Lyla," Dorfman said. "She can't hear herself fart."

But Macklin kept his voice low. "Laurie's divorcing me."

"I'm sorry. Being a criminal attorney, I can't help you. But I can recommend some good divorce men."

"I'm going to settle. I can't afford to have experts performing archaeology on the source of my finances."

"That's wise. Do you have a figure in mind?"

"Half a million should do it. Another hundred for incidentals."

"Have that much?"

"No. That's why I'm here. I need to work."

"What about your legitimate business?"

"I should have sold out ten years ago. No one goes to camera stores any more. Any prospects?"

"I may have something, but you won't like it."

"A name?"

"Sal Malavaggio."

Macklin didn't like it.

"I didn't know he was out," he said.

"He's in a halfway house in the Irish Hills. Next week he'll be back in Detroit. One of his people called. I said I didn't have those contacts any more. I thought you were out of it."

Macklin said nothing. He never wasted time on regrets.

The lawyer said, "Your timing couldn't be better—if you want the job. He wants six guys dead, and he wants it fast. I know you like groundwork, but you'll have to scramble on this one. I think we can get him up to a hundred a pop."

"I need a hundred up front."

"I don't know if he'll agree to that."

"He will. This isn't a job for Costco."

Since he'd moved out of the house in Toledo, Peter Macklin was renting a house in Pontiac, thirty miles northwest of Detroit. When he got back from Redford, he switched on the TV for company. Somebody had blown up something in the Middle East. It seemed to be a big deal.

He wasn't thrilled about working for Salvatore Malavaggio. The man was as Sicilian as they came—his family tree didn't branch— and had done fifteen years on a RICO rap he might have beaten if he'd gone into Witness Protection; but he was an old-school Omerta man, buried so deep in the foundations of the Mafia he flossed his teeth with a garrote.

Macklin had thought to leave that all behind many years ago. After his first divorce he'd gone independent, demanding that prospective clients come up with income tax forms and bank statements detailing everything they owned, which was what he charged for committing murder. This policy weeded out the frivolous. It was amazing how many people were willing to take a vow of poverty just to tip someone the black spot.

Then he'd met Laurie, a beautiful, intelligent woman half his age, and retired on his legitimate investments; but eventually the truth of his past had come out, and that was the end of that.

Now here he was, in his forties, separated, forced to fall back on the only skill he had to survive.

When the FedEx package arrived he took out a small rounded rectangle of plastic.

"Expect it," Dorfman had said. "It's a burn phone, anonymous and untraceable. Throw it in the river when you're through with it. The money will be electronically deposited in the following banks, first the advance, then an additional payment each time you score; nine thousand in each account, so it won't be reported to the IRS. My ten percent comes off the top."

A series of names and account numbers followed, all prearranged for just such a situation. Macklin had written them all down. "We don't meet face to face after today. Wait for instructions by text."

No room for bargaining on the fee. Leo Dorfman was the only lawyer in the country who'd go near the case. It had made him a millionaire many times over, but the other side of the coin was he'd installed a remote starter in his car in case of detonation.

The first text came in ten minutes after Macklin finished charging the phone. Something buzzed, he pressed a key, and looked at the screen. It provided a name, address, vital statistics, and a photo. A second text informed him that ninety thousand dollars had been deposited in his name, spread out among ten separate accounts. It was really amazing what technology had done for crime.

Nikolai Kobolov lived in Bloomfield Village, where a house smaller than 5,000 square feet was considered a starter. When the Berlin

Wall fell and the KGB temporarily lost interest in the Russian Mafia, he'd emigrated to the U.S. and invested his Swiss bank accounts in the insurance business, selling protection to expatriate Communists from their enemies, and occasionally from his own people, who respected such things as Molotov cocktails.

He hung his bullet-shaped body in good tailoring and in the wintertime wore a long belted overcoat and a fur hat, like Omar Sharif in *Doctor Zhivago*. He was part Ukrainian, descended from Cossacks.

When he left his house, riding in the back of a stretch Lincoln driven by a chauffeur in livery, two cars followed, one containing four men licensed to carry firearms in defense of his life. Two FBI agents rode in the other. It was almost four o'clock, the time appointed for his daily shaving. He liked a clean head.

The shop downtown, which called itself a salon, was all glistening glass, chrome, and tile. He took a seat in his customary chair while his bodyguards read newspapers in the waiting area and the two FBI men sat in their car outside. A man Kobolov didn't recognize covered him in crisp white linen. He wore a white jacket fastened at one shoulder with buttons.

"Where's Fred?" the customer asked.

"Sick today."

He shook a thick finger at the man. "No nicks. I'm going out with a young lady tonight."

"Yes, sir." The barber removed a towel from the warmer and wrapped it turbanlike around Kobolov's head. The Russian sighed, lulled into a doze, as always, by the heat. He barely shuddered when the ice pick entered the top of his spinal column. The bodyguards were still reading when the barber went out through the back room.

Sanders Quotient was a third-round draft choice for the Detroit Lions, but he'd been drummed out of the league for unsportsmanlike conduct. He'd sued on the basis of discrimination; however, the NAACP had refused him use of its counsel. He'd invested the proceeds from his first year's contract in one of the biggest drug operations in the Midwest, dealing in cocaine and heroin. Some of it was too strong for the clientele, who'd died of OD.

He lived in an original Frank Lloyd Wright house in St. Clair Shores. The open plan, and the unobstructed view through big windows, appealed to him.

He had no bodyguards. At thirty-five, in excellent condition, he could take care of himself. If that was overoptimistic, he had two DEA agents watching his house in eight-hour shifts, hoping to catch him in an illegal transaction.

He got up around 2:00 A.M., leaving a fine young woman in his round bed, to crack open a bottle of imported beer. In the kitchen, he heard a thump coming from his deck.

On the way through the rec room he selected a Glock nine from the rack and went to the sliding glass door to investigate. Gripping the weapon tightly and hugging the wall, he reached for the lock. It was open. He always made sure everything was sealed tight before bed.

He was turning from the door, pistol in hand, when his head exploded.

The coroner assigned cause of death to a blow that caved in his skull, pieces of which clung by blood and gray matter to a blackjack, discarded without fingerprints.

Zev Issachar controlled most of the illegal gambling between Chicago and the East Coast. At seventy-two, he was retired, but there wasn't an underground casino or unsanctioned high-stakes poker game that didn't pay him tribute. He'd changed his name legally from Howard Needleman before applying for residency in Israel to avoid arrest. Tel Aviv had turned him down.

He was awaiting trial for violation of the laws of interstate commerce. It was a rap he could beat, but he considered the electronic ankle tether humiliating, and it aggravated his arthritis.

On Saturday, he boarded a van belonging to the Justice Department, bound from his modest home in Highland Park to synagogue, in the company of two U.S. deputy marshals. Inside the temple, as his manacles were being removed, a man dressed as a Hassidim shot him three times in the chest before vanishing into the crowd waiting for the inner doors to open. Zev died instantly. The marshals gave chase, but found only a coat, hat, wig, and false whiskers in a pile by the fire exit.

"I thought we'd moved beyond all this after nine-eleven."

Inspector Deborah Stonesmith commanded the Detroit Major Crimes Unit, which was helping to coordinate the efforts of the three major homicide divisions involved. She was a tall, handsome black woman with reddish hair, dressed conservatively in tweeds. The only touch of femininity in her office at 1300 Beaubien, Detroit Police Headquarters, was a spray of peonies in a vase on her desk.

"That's just it." Wes Crider, a homicide lieutenant, lifted a shoulder and let it drop. "These mobsters think we're too busy looking for Islamic Fascists to bother with them."

"They never heard of multitasking? If this is the Russian Mafia taking on the black Mafia, or the Jewish Mafia taking on either of the others, it's a turf war. Targeting all three makes it something else."

"A synagogue, yet; a place of worship. Is nothing sacred?"

"As opposed to plain murder? Who else we got?"

Crider took out a notebook with scraps of ragged paper sticking out of the edges at every angle, like Grandma's cookbook. "Kim Park? Got all the massage parlors nailed down; prostitution, with a little shiatsu on the side. Korean Cosa Nostra."

"He's a maybe. What about Sal Malavaggio? He's a sitting duck in that halfway house. Security there's to keep them in, not others out."

"He's strictly a Mustache Pete. Those Sicilians went out with Pet Rocks."

"Let's put a car out front, just in case. Who else?"

Flip, flip. "Vittorio Bandolero, runs the best restaurant in Mexicantown. Smuggles illegals into the country. Last time his people thought they were being tailed, they machine-gunned the carload."

"Next."

"Jebediah Colt: Jeb the Reb, on the street. Dixie Mafia, Stolen Goods Division. Fences everything from bellybutton rings to catalytic converters."

Stonesmith smiled. "I've seen his file. Sweetbreads in his freezer is what he's got for brains. What else?"

"That's the kit. All the Mafias: Russian, black, Jewish, Asian, Mexican, Dixie, and the Sicilian original. You know, if they'd just trademarked the name—"

"They'd be Microsoft."

"*Sí*, I understand. I, too, would exit the driver's seat of a truck when a helicopter flew overhead; however, I might have waited until a searchlight came on, just to make sure it wasn't a traffic vehicle from a radio station."

Vittorio Bandolero hung up and scowled at the man seated across the desk. They were in the back room of the Mexicantown restaurant whose income he reported to the federal government for taxation purposes. "I am losing patience with Immigration. Not all of my people have the slightest interest in overthrowing the government. I merely want *muchachos* who can fry a tortilla and cut the occasional throat. Is that too much to ask?"

Bandolero's *segundo*, a small man with scars on both cheeks and black hair swept back from his temples—longer than those on top, like the fenders of a 1949 Mercury—moved his shoulders, paring his nails with a switchblade. "There are people to grease, *jefe*. We should meet with them."

"*Dónde?*"

"The Alamo; ten o'clock, so I am told."

The Alamo Motel stood on East Jefferson facing the river, a dump that rented rooms by the hour. Bandolero knocked at the door he'd been directed to. It opened at the pressure of his fist. He stepped inside.

Something swooped, tightened around his throat. He couldn't get his hands under it. He thrashed, crooked his elbows, made no contact. His tongue slid out of his mouth just before he lost consciousness.

The first officer on the scene reported a deceased male, apparently strangled to death with nylon fishline.

Deborah Stonesmith stood over the body of Vittorio Bandolero, dragged into a sitting position against the wall of the motel room. The fishline was embedded two inches into his neck.

"No more Mr. Nice Guy," she said. "Someone's moving in."

Lieutenant Crider said, "We need to open a tip line. An army of hit men can't go unnoticed for long."

"So it's an army."

"We got us an ice pick, a bludgeon, a gun, and a garrote. Heavy-lifters specialize. Nobody uses this much variety."

"One does," she said, smoothing her tweed skirt. "I thought he was dead, or moved—or hoped so; but wishful thinking never got nobody nothing but thinking wishful."

Kim Park had come to the U.S. with a dollar eighty-seven in his pocket; also three hundred thousand dollars in Krugerrands in the false bottom of his suitcase, belonging to a Detroit politician who died before taking delivery. Park had invested this windfall in a string of massage parlors. He found America truly to be the Land of Opportunity.

The girls were skilled. What did it matter if their trained hands were joined by their bodies, so long as they split the tips with the management? But then an undercover cop had found a girl willing to testify that she'd been sold into slavery by her parents. She'd managed to stumble into a number of Dumpsters between Detroit and Flint: her torso here, a leg there, and her head and hands who knew where. A man couldn't be held responsible for the bad choices of all his employees.

In any case, Kim Park never went anywhere without a train of vice officers making note of where he stopped and whom he spoke to. It pleased him to think of them stuck in their cars while he took a steam in one of his own places in Detroit.

He'd just poured a dipper of water over the heated rocks when the door opened, stirring the thick vapor. He grinned, expecting a half-naked Korean girl ready to escort him to the table. His head was still wearing the grin when it rolled out of the steam room, cut off with a hunting knife found in a towel hamper, its handle wiped clean.

Sal Malavaggio selected a cigar from the humidor on his desk, rustled it next to his ear, dropped it back into the box, and shut the lid. "Remind me to order fresh cigars. *I* kept better than these did."

"Way ahead of you," Miriam Brewster said. "A colleague in Key West has a standing order of Montecristos. Two boxes on the way."

Malavaggio, short and stout, with a glossy head of dyed-black hair, had chosen Brewster out of vanity; she was an inch shorter than he was, and fatter yet in a tailored suit. But she had turned out to be a double blessing as one of the country's foremost Constitutional scholars.

"Tell me again about overturning RICO." He settled himself in the upholstered leather chair, taking in the comforts of home for the first time in fifteen years.

She sat facing the desk and crossed her chubby legs. "It will take years, and maybe a change or two on the Supreme Court, but anyone can tell you it's a jump-wire around the Bill of Rights. The government couldn't get your people legally, so it crooked the system. In a way it was a victory for you."

"Yeah. That brought me comfort in stir, while them animals took over the works. Russian Mafia, black Mafia, Jewish Mafia, Asian Mafia. They couldn't even come up with a name of their own. But I'm changing that."

He looked at his Rolex, lifted a remote off the desk, and snapped it at the new flatscreen TV mounted on the wall opposite. A local reporter stood in front of one of Kim Park's rub-a-dub parlors, chattering breathlessly as morgue attendants carried a body bag on a stretcher out the door. "Trouble with whacking a chink," Malavaggio said, "an hour later you want to whack another one."

"I didn't hear that." Brewster's lips were tight. "Be patient, Sal, I beg you. What good's winning our point when you're doing life for murder?"

"What murder's that, Counselor? I was checking out of the halfway house when some *feccia* made that improvement in Jackie Chan's looks. Same place I was when the Russky bought it, and the porch monkey and the Hebe. Sounds like the start of a joke, don't it? They go into a bar?"

"Sure, Sal. You're clean."

"Cleaning house," he said. "When I'm through, everybody'll know there's only one Mafia."

Colt's Ponies sold campers, travel trailers, and motor homes from four locations in the Detroit metropolitan area. The business provided an income Jebediah Colt could declare on his taxes and a neat bit of camouflage: Who'd look for a trailer containing hot transmissions on a trailer lot?

He'd declared his independence at fourteen, when he cold-cocked his father with a meat hammer, stole a car, and drove north to assemble Mustangs at Ford River Rouge. He was fired for stealing tools and parts, but by then he'd put enough away to open his own full-time business at twenty. He dealt in jewelry, rare coins, copper plumbing, and genuine factory auto parts, all stolen.

He hadn't much overhead. All you needed was a roof, preferably one with wheels; that way, when you got the tip a raid was coming, all you had to do was hitch up and move to another lot. Now he owned a fleet of Mustangs he hadn't had a thing to do with in the manufacture and a house in Grosse Pointe, down the street from the Ford family itself.

"Mr. Colt? Deborah Stonesmith. I'm an inspector with the Detroit Police Department." The tall black woman who'd rung his doorbell showed him a shield.

"You got a warrant?"

"I'm not here to arrest you. I assume you've heard about the recent gangland killings."

He grinned his baggy grin, scratched the tattoo on his upper left arm. "No shit, you're here to *protect* me?"

"We've got a car on this block, an early response team in radio contact, and a man on each side of the house. I'm going to ask you to stay in tonight. Since this business started, no more than two nights have passed between killings. This is the third since Kim Park's."

His smile vanished. "That pimp? What's the connection?"

"We think someone's out to eliminate the competition in organized crime in the area. You and Salvatore Malavaggio are the only honchos left. My lieutenant is at Sal's place in Birmingham, explaining these same arrangements."

"Well, I'm expecting delivery of an Airstream at my lot in Belleville, straight from the factory. I like to be there when something new comes in."

"You can inspect your swag another time, Jeb. Either that, or we'll send a car to follow you; for your own safety, of course."

Macklin spotted the early response van first thing. The panels advertised a diaper service, a stork in a messenger's cap with a little bundle of joy strung from its beak. There wasn't a playset or a bicycle or anything else on the block that indicated a resident young enough to have small children. He drove past, located the unmarked car containing two plainclothesmen drinking Starbucks across the street from Colt's house, and saw flashlight beams prowling the grounds.

A big-box department store stood near downtown, connected with a service station. He bought a two-gallon gasoline can, put in a quart from the pump, stashed it in his trunk, and entered the store. In the liquor section he put a liter bottle of inexpensive wine into his basket. Browsing in entertainment, he came upon a James Brown retrospective on CD and a cheap player. He bought them at the front counter, along with a package of batteries and a disposable lighter from the impulse rack.

The restrooms were located inside the foyer. Finding the men's room empty, he unscrewed the cap from the wine bottle and dumped the contents down the sink. In the parking lot he opened his trunk, the lid blocking the view from the security camera mounted on a light pole, filled the bottle with gasoline, replaced the cap, wrapped it in an old shirt he used for a rag, tucked the bundle under his arm inside his jacket, slammed the trunk, got into the car, and drove away.

Three blocks from Jebediah Colt's house, a FOR SALE sign stood in the yard of a brick split-level on a corner. The inside was dark except for a tiny steady red light.

There were no security cameras visible. He walked up to the front door and rang the bell; a househunter, hoping to catch someone at home. When no one answered after the second ring, he produced the CD player from under his coat, placed it on the doorstep, and switched it on, turning up the volume until James Brown's lyrics were distorted beyond comprehension. He returned to the car, moving quickly now, drove around the corner, opened the gasoline-filled bottle, spilled a little onto a piece he'd torn off the old shirt, stuffed the rag into the neck, and lit it with the disposable lighter. When it was burning, he opened the driver's window and slung the bottle at the nearest window. The security alarm went off shrilly.

The bottle exploded with a whump and the flame spread. He drove away at a respectable speed, hearing the Godfather of Soul screaming at the top of his lungs from the direction of the burning house.

Police on stakeout might ignore a house fire, expecting local units and the fire department to take care of it; but someone screaming in the flames was another story. The early response team reported the hysterical noises over the radio, and within five minutes Jeb "the Reb" Colt was a man alone.

The sirens started up with a whoop, loud enough to make him jump up from in front of the NASCAR channel and draw aside his front curtains. The noises were fading away. He got his nunchuks from the drawer, turned off the lights to avoid being framed in the doorway, and stepped onto his front porch.

He saw an orange glow three blocks away and lights going on in his neighbors' houses. Shrugging, he swung the chuks together in his fist and turned to go inside. Someone stood between him and the doorway. The heel of a hand swept up, driving bone splinters from his nose into his brain.

Miriam Brewster switched off the flatscreen and turned to Malavaggio, leaning back in his desk chair with his pudgy hands folded across his broad stomach and his lids drifted nearly shut. He looked like a toad. "I don't suppose you know anything about this."

"The arson? Insurance job, probably. Guy can't keep up his mortgage, he torches the place for case dough."

"I mean Jeb Colt."

"One cracker more or less don't mean much to the world."

"You must have squirreled away plenty before you went to prison. Six hits in ten days, all professionally done. That doesn't come cheap, even on double-coupon days."

"Even so, I arranged a discount. Why pay for finished work? What's he going to repossess?"

She made him stop before sharing any details.

Macklin had several ways of knowing when someone had entered his house when he was gone. Whoever it was, cop or killer, had stumbled on the one least subtle, forgetting which lights he'd left on and which he'd turned off. He didn't even have to stop his car. The windows told him everything.

In the crowded parking lot of a cineplex, he used his burn phone one last time to call Leo Dorfman.

"How'd he know where I live?" he asked.

The lawyer didn't ask who. "I never told him; but his outfit's got its thumbs in lots of places, why not realty agencies?"

"I need to have been somewhere else when most of those packages were delivered."

"Most, or all?"

"All would look like planning. I can tell 'em I went to the movies for the others."

"Okay."

The parking lot exit passed over an ornamental bridge leading to the highway. Macklin threw the phone out the window into the swift little stream.

Dorfman would take care of the cops; if it was cops. If it was a killer, all he had to do was cut off the source of income.

Salvatore Malavaggio snipped the end off a crisp Montecristo, got it going with a platinum lighter, and blew a smoke ring at the acoustical ceiling in his home office. It had been a good first week out of stir. The Russian, the black, the Jew, the Mexican, the chink, and the hillbilly were gone, leaving a void only an experienced don could fill. His former associates would know the truth. There would be some resistance, but he'd struck too fast and too deep not to have put the fear of Sal into them all. Even Miriam, as cold-blooded a dame as he'd known, had looked at him with new respect after the mug shots of all six rivals appeared on the TV report capping recent events.

There was only one Mafia. There was no room in it for Slavs, coloreds, kikes, greasers, chinks, or inbred morons. Those outsiders only got such big ideas when the Sicilians became careless and gave incriminating orders direct to unreliable street soldiers instead of going through buffers. Malavaggio had used Dorfman, never laying eyes on this Macklin, who was familiar by reputation. The law, too, would know what happened, but it could never prove a connection, no matter what the chump said when he was arrested.

Which was how they'd done things in the old country. *Omerta* was for equals only.

From now on, if you couldn't point at that island off the toe of the boot and name the birthplace of every one of your ancestors, you're just the guy we send out for coffee. *Napolitano?* Ha! *Calabrese?* As if! *Sola Siciliana, per sempre.*

Something clinked in the next room: Miriam, setting down the latest of who knew how many glasses of his best grappa. He hoped she wasn't turning into a lush. She needed all her senses to get the Supreme Court to act and return *La Cosa Nostra* to its days of glory.

And he'd saved himself a hundred grand.

Something stirred in the connecting doorway.

"Counselor? Thought you went home."

"She did. I waited to make sure she didn't come back for something she forgot."

Malavaggio didn't recognize the man coming in carrying a revolver. They'd never met face to face.

# The Tree on Execution Hill

*This is my first published short story. It appeared in* Alfred Hitchcock's Mystery Magazine *in 1977, not long after my first novel was published. At the time I'd just started my last newspaper job, in my hometown of Dexter, Michigan, so the setting was fresh daily.*

It seemed as if everybody in Good Advice had turned out for the meeting that night in the town hall. Every seat was taken, and the dark oaken rafters resounded with a steady hum of conversation while the broad pine planks that made up the floor creaked beneath the tread of many feet.

Up in front, his plaid jacket thrown back to expose a generous paunch, Carl Lathrop, the town's leading storekeeper and senior member of the council, stood talking with Birdie Flatt from the switchboard. His glasses flashed a Morse code in the bright overhead lights as he settled and resettled them on his fleshy nose. I recognized the gesture from the numerous interviews I had conducted with him as a sign that he was feeling very satisfied with himself, and so I knew what was coming long before most of my neighbors expected it.

I was something of a freak in the eyes of the citizenry of Good Advice, New Mexico. This was partly because I had been the first person to settle in the area since before 1951, when the aircraft plant had moved on to greener pastures, and partly because, at forty-two, I was at least ten years younger than anyone else in town. Most people supposed I stayed on out of despair after my wife Sylvia left me to return to civilization, but that wasn't strictly true. We'd originally planned to lay over for a week or two while I collected information for my book and then move on. But then the owner of the town newspaper had died and the paper was put up for sale, and I bought it with the money we'd saved up for the trip. It had been an act of impulse, perhaps a foolish one—so far away from her beloved beauty parlors—but my chief fear in life had always been that I'd miss the big opportunity when it came along. So now I had a newspaper but no Sylvia, which, all things considered, seemed a pretty fair trade.

The buzz of voices died out as Lathrop took his place behind the lectern. I flipped open my notebook and sat with pencil poised to capture any pearls of wisdom he might have been about to drop.

"We all know why we're here, so we'll dispense with the long-winded introductions." A murmur of approval rippled through the audience. "You've all heard the rumor that the state may build a superhighway near Good Advice," he went on. "Well, it's my pleasant duty to announce that it's no longer a rumor."

Cheers and applause greeted this statement, and it was some minutes before the room grew quiet enough for Lathrop to continue.

"Getting information out of these government fellows is like pulling teeth," he said. "But after about a dozen phone calls to the capital, I finally got hold of the head of the contracting firm that's going to do the job. He told me they plan to start building sometime next fall." He waited until the fresh applause faded, then went on. "Now, this doesn't mean that Good Advice is going to become another Santa Fe overnight. When those tourists come streaming in here, we're going to have to be ready for them. That means rezoning for tourist facilities, fixing up our historic landmarks, and so on. The reason we called this meeting is to decide on ways to make this town appealing to visitors. The floor is open to suggestions."

I spent the next twenty minutes jotting down some of the ideas that came from the enthusiastic citizens. Birdie Flatt was first, with a suggestion that the telephone service be updated, but others disagreed, maintaining that the old upright phones and wall installations found in many of the downtown shops added to the charm of the town. "Uncle Ned" Scoffield, at ninety-seven Good Advice's oldest resident, offered to clean out and fix up the old trading post at the end of Main Street in return for permission to sell his wood carvings and his collection of handwoven Navajo rugs. Carl Lathrop pledged to turn the old jail, which he had been using as a storeroom, into a tourist attraction. The fact that outlaw Ford Harper had spent his last days there before his hanging, he said, could only add to its popularity.

Then, amidst a chorus of groans from scattered parts of the room, Avery Sharecross stood up.

Sharecross was a spindly scarecrow of a man, with an unkempt mane of lusterless black hair spilling over the collar of his frayed sweater and a permanent stoop that made him appear much older than he was. Nobody in town could say how he made his living. Certainly not from the bookstore he had been operating on the corner of Main and Maple for thirty years; there were never any more than two customers in the store at a time, and the prices he charged were so ridiculously low that it was difficult to believe he managed to break even, let alone show a profit. Everyone was aware of the monthly pension he received from an address in Santa Fe, but no one knew how much it was or why he got it. His bowed shoulders and shuffling gait, the myopia that forced him to squint through the thick tinted lenses of his eyeglasses, the hollows in his pale cheeks were as much a part of the permanent scenery in Good Advice as the burned-out shell of the old flour mill north of town. I closed my notebook and put away my pencil, knowing what he was going to talk about before he opened his mouth. It was all he ever talked about.

Lathrop sighed. "What is it, Avery? As if I didn't know." He rested his chin on one pudgy hand, bracing himself for the ordeal.

"Mr. Chairman, I have a petition." The old bookseller rustled the well-thumbed sheaf of papers he held in one talonlike hand. "I have twenty-six signatures demanding that the citizens of Good Advice vote on whether the tree on Execution Hill be removed."

There was an excited buzz among the spectators. I sat bolt upright in my chair, flipping my notebook back open. How had the old geezer got twenty-five people to agree with him?

For 125 years the tree in question had dominated the high-domed hill two miles outside town, its skeletal limbs stretching naked against the sky. Of the eighteen trials that had been held in the town hall during the nineteenth century, eleven of those tried had ended up swinging from the tree's stoutest limb. It was a favorite spot of mine, an excellent place to sit and meditate. Avery Sharecross, for reasons known only to himself, had been trying to get the council to destroy it for five years. This was the first time he had not stood alone.

Lathrop cleared his throat loudly, probably to cover up his own astonishment. "Now, Avery, you know as well as I do that it takes fifty-five signatures on a petition to raise a vote. You've read the charter."

Sharecross was unperturbed.

"When that charter was drafted, Mr. Chairman, this town boasted a population of over fourteen hundred. In the light of our present count, I believe that provision can be waived." He struck the pages with his fingertips. "These signatures represent nearly one-tenth of the local electorate. They have a right to be heard."

"How come you're so fired up to see that tree reduced to kindling, anyway? What's the difference to you?"

"That tree"—Sharecross flung a scrawny arm in the direction of the nearest window—"represents a time in this town's history when lynch law reigned and pompous hypocrites sentenced their peers to death regardless of their innocence or guilt." His cheeks were flushed now, his eyes ablaze behind the bottle-glass spectacles. "That snarl of dead limbs has been a blemish on the smooth face of this community for over a hundred years, and it's time we got rid of it."

It was an impressive performance, and he sounded sincere, but I wasn't buying it. Good Advice, after all, had not been my first exposure to journalism. After you've been in this business a while, you get a feeling for when someone is telling the truth. Sharecross wasn't.

Whatever reasons he had for wishing to destroy the town's oldest landmark, they had nothing to do with any sense of injustice. Of that I was certain.

Lathrop sighed. "All right, Avery, let's see your petition. If the signatures check out, we'll vote."

Once the papers were in his hand, Lathrop called the other members of the town council around him to look them over. Finally he motioned them back to their seats and turned back toward the lectern. For the next half-hour he read off the names on the petition—many of which surprised me, for they included some of the town's leading citizens—to make sure the signatures were genuine. Every one of those mentioned spoke up to assure him they were. At length the storekeeper laid the pages down.

"Before we vote," he said, "the floor is open to dissenting opinions. Mr. Manning?"

My hand had gone up before he finished speaking. I got to my feet, conscious of all the eyes upon me.

"No one is arguing what Mr. Sharecross said about the injustices done in the past," I began haltingly. "But tearing down something that's a large part of our history won't change anything."

I paused, searching for words. I was a lot more eloquent in front of a typewriter. "Mr. Sharecross says the tree reminds us of the sordid past. I think that's as it should be. A nagging reminder of a time when we weren't so noble is a healthy thing to have in our midst. I wouldn't want to live in a society that kicked its mistakes under the rug."

The words were coming easier now. "There's been a lot of talk here tonight about promoting tourist trade. Well, destroying a spot where eleven infamous badmen met their rewards is one sure way of aborting any claims we might have had upon shutter-happy visitors." I shook my head emphatically, a gesture left over from my college debate club days. "History is too precious for us to turn our backs on it, for whatever reason. Sharecross and his sympathizers would do well to realize that our true course calls for us to turn our gaze forward and forget about rewriting the past."

There was some applause as I sat down, but it died out when Sharecross seized the floor again.

"I'm not a Philistine, Mr. Chairman," he said calmly. "Subject to the will of the council, I hereby pledge the sum of five thousand dollars for the erection of a statue of Enoch Howard, Good Advice's founder, atop Execution Hill once the tree has been removed. I, too, have some feeling for history." His eyes slid my direction.

That was dirty pool, I thought as he took his seat amid thunderous cheering. In one way or another, Enoch Howard's blood flowed in the veins of over a third of the population of Good Advice. Now I knew how he'd obtained those signatures.

But why? What did he hope to gain?

"Who's going to pay to take down the tree?" someone asked.

Sharecross rose again. "Floyd Kramer there has offered to dig it out by the roots with his backhoe free of charge. All he wants is permission to sell it for firewood."

"That true, Floyd?" Lathrop asked.

A heavy-jowled man in a blue work shirt buttoned to the neck gave him the high sign from his standing position near the door.

I shot out of my chair again, but this time my eyes were directed on my skeletal opponent and not the crowd. "I've fought you in print and on the floor of the town hall over this issue," I said, "and if necessary I'll keep on fighting you all the way to the top of Execution Hill. I don't care how many statues you pull out of your hat; you won't get your way."

The old bookseller made no reply. His eyes were blank behind his spectacles. I sat back down.

I could see that Lathrop's attitude had changed, for he had again taken to raising and lowering his eyeglasses confidently on the bridge of his nose. Enoch Howard was his great-grandfather on his mother's side. "Now we'll vote," he said. "All those in favor of removing the tree on Execution Hill to make room for a statue of our city's founder signify by saying aye."

Rain was hissing on the grass when I parked my battered pickup truck at the bottom of the hill and got out to fetch the shovel out of the back. It was a long climb to the top and I was out of shape, but I didn't want to risk leaving telltale ruts behind by driving up the slope. Halfway up, my feet began to feel like lead and the blood was pounding in my ears like a pneumatic hammer; by the time I reached the base of the tree I had barely enough energy left to find the spot I wanted and begin digging. It was dark, and the soil was soaked just enough so that each time I took out a shovelful the hole filled up with mud. It was ten minutes before I made any progress at all. After half an hour I stopped to rest. That's when all the lights came on and turned night into day.

The headlights of half a dozen automobiles were trained full upon me. For a fraction of a second I stood frozen with shock. Then I hurled the shovel like a javelin at the nearest light and started to run.

The first step I took landed in the hole. I fell headlong to the ground, emptying my lungs and twisting my ankle. When I looked up I was surrounded by people.

"I've waited five years for this." The voice belonged to Avery Sharecross.

I found my breath then. "How did you know?"

"I never did. Not for sure." He was standing over me now, an avenging angel wearing a threadbare coat and scarf. "I once heard that you spent every cent you had on the newspaper. If that was true, I wondered what your wife used for bus fare back to Santa Fe when she left you. Everyone knew you argued with her bitterly over your decision to stay. That you lost control and murdered her seemed obvious to me.

"I decided you buried her by the hanging tree. That explained why you spent so much more time here than anyone else. Probably you needed the reassurance that she was still where you'd left her.

"Well, I wasn't going to dig up the whole hill all by myself, so it became necessary to catch you in the act. That's when I got the idea to push for removing the tree and force you to move the body."

He turned to a tall man whose Stetson glistened wetly in the unnatural illumination of the headlights at his back. "Sheriff, if your men will resume digging where Mr. Manning left off, it's my guess you'll find the corpse of Sylvia Manning before midnight. I retired from the Santa Fe Police Department long before they were required to read suspects their rights, so perhaps you'll oblige."

# Sincerely, Mr. Hyde

*Thanks to Robert Louis Stevenson for inspiring this one. One definition of a classic is there's always something new you can bring to it.*

This is my suicide note.

It's all Jekyll's doing, feeble prig that he is; his infernal decency has begun to engulf me, just when I thought my logic was bringing him round. Sometime as I slept coiled inside him, he smuggled in a conscience.

Monstrous vandalism, that, like throwing paint on a Greek statue. (Inspired mischief: Is the British Museum open at this hour?) I was unique among my fellow *Homo sapiens*, a man thoroughly without scruple, a pure thing.

Jekyll's greatest creation, surpassing God.

The poison—tincture of arsenic and strychnine, with a dash of potassium cyanide, a most lethal postprandial libation—awaits me in a measured beaker, looking quite benign in comparison with the elixir of my release, glowing and foaming bilious green as it does when the powder is introduced, like sulfur dissolved in essence of mad dog.

Soon the world will know the truth: that Henry Jekyll and Edward Hyde are one and the same, saint and sinner, philanthropist and murderer, saver and taker of lives.

But I'm Hyde yet. If the pang becomes unendurable, I'll anesthetize it with gin.

How well I remember my birth, unlike those born of woman: my creator writhing in agony while I tore myself from his insides in impatient rage; my face in the cheval-glass, all ridges and bone and swollen eyeballs, dripping with amniotic fluid like a child just delivered. All babies are ugly at the start, red and wrinkled, their faces distended with wrath. No one had consulted them on the matter of their birth, or warned them what to expect when they still had the chance to strangle themselves with their umbilical cords. All mankind is born angry.

Just how Jekyll came to christen me Edward Hyde is a mystery. "Edward" is easy: An uncle of that name died in an asylum for the criminally insane, after chopping up his wife and four children with a hatchet. I am his direct descendant. "Hyde" is enigmatic: Am I the sordid thing that crawls beneath the hide of all humanity, or the dreaded thing from which all humanity must hide?

Or he may simply have come upon the inspiration sitting on a bench in Hyde Park. The damn absent-minded scientist is easily distracted by the course of his thoughts. Just because we share the same knowledge and memories does not mean we can follow the circumlocution of a highly educated mind.

It's my mind, too, don't forget. I benefit from Jekyll's many years of study and practise, without having had to fidget in the lecture-hall, the laboratory, and the dissection room, redolent of ammonia, formaldehyde, and raw human flesh; although I revel in that last sense-memory. The extinction of life is the essence of art. I slew a man in Hampstead for dipping snuff. Filthy habit; but he died well. I ate his heart.

Henry—for I am certainly close enough to him to address him by his Christian name—has never appreciated his good fortune: In this third decade of the reign of good Queen Victoria, to sample the exquisite pleasures of the London *demimonde*—more extensive in their delicious variety than in all of Sodom—while maintaining one's respectable reputation, must surely be the dream of any man with blood in his veins.

I gave him that gift; but to what end? Loathed, hunted, held in deepest contempt by the man who bore me, and now consigned to execution by that same revered practitioner. I would throttle him with my bare hands if it wouldn't serve his purpose as well as the poison.

O, but to experience just once more the abandon of Limehouse, Spitalfields, the music-halls where ribald comedies play out onstage while even greater entertainment takes place in the boxes above, swaddled in curtains; opium dens, brothels, cockfights in Soho, bear-baiting in the Isle of Dogs. I lost a good deal of Henry's fortune on a grizzly named Lord Bartholomew, but made it back on a mastiff they called Geronimo; then blew it on a virgin in a Greenwich bordello who turned out not to be as advertised. I strangled the madam to death with one of her own elbow-length gloves. I despise misrepresentation.

Nothing came of that, as no one cares about such creatures; but as happens in the course of things, something far more trivial set events against me.

It wasn't the boy at the West India docks, for I paid him handsomely in return for his silence; nor even the vagabond I doused with coal-oil and touched off with a match in Soho. They didn't even make the *Telegraph*. An anarchist bombing in the Underground drove them square off the columns.

I wonder just how one goes about constructing a bomb? Black powder is easily obtained, fuses and timers even more so; and books on the subject are available in certain places with which I'm familiar. I should like to blow up the Tower, at a peak time when all the tourists are filing past the crowned jewels, the blood and entrails of the innocent commingling with the baubles of the privileged few. But I suppose that's an impossible dream now.

No, it was a trifling affair that undid me, scarcely worth including in one's memoirs. A filthy little girl in pinafores ran square into me on my way home from a public-house, long after the hour when such creatures should be in bed. I stomped her, of course. There happened to be witnesses present—busybodies, who ought to mind to their own affairs—and I was forced by sheer numbers to retreat to Henry's laboratory and scribble out a cheque for some petty amount in the way of repairs—contusions and abrasions, that's all the thing was about. Given time, I'd have put the little baggage in crutches for life. But everything can be bought off, even indignation. The worst consequence was I'd been identified in connection with my dear benefactor.

The incident worked on Henry. I wonder if that precious conscience of his is at all diminished by sharing some of it with me. In any event he laid off the drug that led to my delivery for months.

Guv'nor, have you ever spent months in confinement, separated by iron bars from your true nature? Well, the Jekyll in me—curse the prude—hopes you never will.

I'd have none of it. When first he made my acquaintance, I was nearly a dwarf, stunted by decades of repression. Now, having feasted on the septet of sins, I stood close to his height. I'd grown too strong to remain incarcerated by anything so juvenile as temperance.

But attaining liberty was no small challenge. Henry was a man to keep vigil. As long as I was in his thoughts, I might as well have been in chains.

Well, even a genius needs to sleep; or relax his guard and slip into a daydream. And Edward Hyde has no need of rest. Evil feeds upon itself, like a mushroom growing in the dark.

I sprang forth as he sat on a public bench, ruminating; a dim silly memory of his mother giving him a biscuit for some darling act of sweetness on his part. I might have vomited if I hadn't been waiting for just that moment. He had time, in the instant before the transformation was complete, to register shock and horror: He'd fallen into his repose a man erect and clean-shaven, nails pared, an exemplar of civilisation, and awoke bent and hirsute, a brute from an age of savagery and stone, where men took their pleasures with club and spear.

I was as a wild horse unbridled; a lion, rather, suddenly released from its cage. I charged across the heath, coattails flying, swinging my stick to open a path through the strolling sluggards standing between me and the orgies I craved. How well I remember their faces changing from annoyance to fear when they looked upon mine, black with engorged blood and white with gnashing teeth.

Storming across a revoltingly charming footbridge, I came upon a stranger, immaculately attired for the evening, with snow-white whiskers. He tipped his hat and bade me good evening.

Had he said nothing and stepped aside, he might have been spared. The mere kindness of his diction drove me to fury. I bludgeoned him to death.

How he pleaded for mercy! How he mewled when the gold knob of Jekyll's stick broke his skull. When the blood spurted from his lips, I'd have gladly shattered every bone in his body. But by then he was inexorably dead; his eyes stared sightless at what I have to own was a sky sprinkled beautifully with stars.

I am an unfortunate man.

The fellow I'd killed was a member of Parliament, one Sir Danvers Carew, and to put the fine point upon it happened to be popular with both the voters and the press. He was a generous donor to charities; of all things for a politician to be.

And I'd been seen.

By a fool housemaid, mooning in a window, who'd observed me well enough in the gaslight to provide an accurate description for Scotland Yard.

So I went underground, into the safe house of the body of Dr. Henry Jekyll.

Understand, my memories were his. He was fully aware of what I'd done, and of his own complicity in keeping it secret. O, I know my Henry, better than he knows himself. He would never condone my conduct, but neither would he expose it, lest it reflect upon himself. I ask you, who is the hypocrite here?

I blended the ingredients of the elixir from memory and crawled back under his skin. The old agony was now nearly gone. Hyde slid into Jekyll, and Jekyll into Hyde, as easily as a button passing through a worn eyelet.

And like that button it slid out just as easily, and at the most inopportune times; but we were both unaware of that as yet.

I lay doggo for a while, as who would not? Safe in the carapace of the good Henry Jekyll, setting the broken bones and draining the pus of the poor, pooh-poohing their gratitude whilst reveling in it; pretending there had never been little naughty Eddie inside noble Hank since Cain slew Abel. No man had ever invented a better place of concealment. I was the luckiest scoundrel ever born—had I been born.

Was it a mistake to leave the broken half of Henry's own stick at the scene of the murder of Sir Danvers Carew? Or did I want to implicate him?

Does anyone care? I hate the man. I would never have existed but for him.

I am back inside him now, but we can both feel the restorative wearing off. My accursed strength is the culprit. He fears to leave the laboratory lest the most wanted criminal in London should suddenly appear in the middle of Piccadilly.

He blames the impurity in the original powder, which can't be duplicated, for his inability to maintain his original identity. What he doesn't understand—which I do, as his Greater Understanding— is he *prefers* to remain Edward Hyde. I'm younger, to begin with, having appeared late in his awakening, and I have delicacies yet to taste, virgins to deflower, innocents to sully, purses to pinch, banks to rob, dogs to kick, and kittens to drown. We could own the Empire, would we just put decency aside. All he must do to banish me to limbo is confess his humanity.

This he will never do.

The beaker stands, in appearance no more prepossessing than a pint of beer in a friendly pub. Peace awaits upon the consumption. He reaches for it.

But before he can grasp it, his hand is covered with coarse hair and ropy veins. It's the hand of a murderer. It closes into a fist and draws away.

Not yet, Henry. Not just yet.

A gentleman keeps his appointments.

I have an assignation in Whitechapel, with a comely piece named Mary Kelly, a delectable flame-haired daughter of Erin, and available for a shilling. She's far more fetching than the others I've encountered in that neighbourhood. I'm unable to use my name now; events beyond the control of us both have forced me to be circumspect.

She knows me only as Jack.

# You Owe Me

*I never pass up the opportunity to write about Depression-era crime. My first novel,* The Oklahoma Punk *(terrible title, forced on me by the publisher; I've retitled it* Red Highway *in all subsequent editions), was my first foray into that territory. I doubt "You Owe Me" will be my last.*

Robbing banks is a tough habit to break.

I've got the old itch; disaster whispering in my ear, its lips warm as a woman's. I get stiff as a fencepost just thinking about it.

It's been months since South Bend. Gigantic foul-up that it was, with too many heroes and that gun-silly Nelson shooting up half the town, I'm ready to go again. My face is about healed, except for some puffiness around the eyes, and in the mirror I look like a cousin of mine a couple of times removed. I doubt even Pop would know me at first glance. Doc Cassidy does good work.

As he should, for the money.

This being on the lam is costly. I don't recommend it, unless you've got cash in the bank; but I don't recommend that, either.

I just might take it.

They call me "John the Killer" in the *Literary Digest*—a rag I'd never have gotten into under normal circumstances. Which is a raw deal. I only killed one person, a cop, and he shot me first.

The name didn't stick, though; no one else uses it. Of all the Baby Faces, Pretty Boys, Mad Dogs, and Machine-Guns this and that, I'm the only bandit known almost exclusively by his last name. "Dillinger" in a headline is enough to sell out several editions.

Public Enemy Number One; that stuck, and how. But it isn't really a nickname, now, is it?

I'll need three things.

The car's easy. I can boost one off the street or grab a brand-new demonstrator from a dealership, like in Greencastle. Guns are more challenging, but if I drive around long enough I'll see the Stars and

Stripes hanging from a pole and do some shopping in a National Guard armory. I keep a .45 handy for just such errands.

A crew, that's something else. Nelson, Van Meter, Charley Floyd are scattered all over the forty-eight, and the screws in Indiana are measuring Handsome Harry for the hot seat. That means a trip to St. Paul and the mail drop there to see if the others have left any word. You can't stick up a bank alone.

You need a man at the door, preferably with a chopper, a man to clean out the vault, someone outside for crowd control, and a wheel, the best you can find. Two or three more top hands, just for insurance. They don't come cheap, so all this guff you hear about John Dillinger's hidden loot is strictly for *Dime Detective*. It goes out almost as fast as it comes in. If anyone had told me how expensive it is to live the Life of Crime, I'd have trained for the stock market; it's just as crooked, but the risks are less fatal.

Not that I'd choose that route. I'd rather go down in a hail of lead than molder away in some office, waiting for my heart to blow out.

I'm at least partly to blame for all the bother.

They didn't install all those time locks and solid oak tellers' cages to keep out a hick like Clyde Barrow and his slutty gal-pal, that's certain. And if I put any more armed guards to work I'll clear up the Depression single-handed. I should be with FDR's Brain Trust.

But I don't do it for the money.

Sure, I like twenty-dollar shirts, suits cut to my build, a legit new car every few months for joy-riding, room service in St. Paul—a good old town where the graft's reasonable so they mostly let you alone—and a fat roll in my pocket; but I'd knock over the brokest bank in Podunk for no more than you'd get from a cash register in a Piggly Wiggly, just for kicks.

Regrets? Some; I wish I'd kept my head that time in East Chicago. Nelson thinks a day without killing is a day wasted, but not me. That poor sap was just doing what they paid him for, and not enough in these times. I miss Billie, my one-and-only. That midget Purvis locked her up after Little Bohemia, just for hanging around with me. Little Bohemia, I regret that one major-league; though not as much, I bet, as the G-men who put us wise by opening fire on a group of law-abiding fishermen, thinking it was the "Terror Gang."

I wish my mother didn't die when I was three.

I'd do a lot of things different, given half the chance. But I don't regret not being a straight.

In 1923, I knocked a greengrocer over the head and stole his roll. They said if I turned myself in, the judge would go easy on me. They said I wouldn't even need a lawyer. I was twenty years old. I was thirty when I got out of the Indiana State Penitentiary.

*You* support these jokers; you make them possible.

You owe me ten years' wages; counting penalties and interest, you're deep in the red.

I met useful people in the Michigan City pen: Bankrobbers who'd worked out all the wrinkles, based on past mistakes. No one ever learned anything from his successes. I can quote Dale Carnegie on that.

That was just fourteen months ago, but I've been busy ever since.

A year ago May I was just another ex-con, dumped out into the middle of an economic emergency. Now I'm more famous than Babe Ruth. Even that crumb Hitler knows my name: He says America's chock-full of gangsters like John Dillinger.

I'm no gangster. They're foreigners, Eye-ties and Micks, stirring up illegal booze in bathtubs and gunning down one another in the streets; and God help the innocent that wanders into the crossfire. Me, I go where the money is and take it straight from the source, just like Jesse James. All clean and straightforward: Robin Hood, if he had V-8 Fords and General Thompson's gun. Imagine what Billy the Kid could do with those.

I'll never get shut of the stink of that craphole in Michigan City. I sure as hell am never going back. That's why I didn't hang around Crown Point any longer than I had to.

Truth to tell, though, that bust-out was almost as much fun as pushing in a First National.

I walked square into the arms of the cops in Tucson like a dumb cluck. You can put that one on my list of things I'd do different. They flew me back to Indiana; only time I was ever in a plane. I didn't enjoy the experience. I thought they were going to dump me out at a thousand feet and save the state the expense of an electric bill.

But I survived, to cool my heels in the Crown Point Jail awaiting trial for the murder of a sheriff in Lima, which wasn't even my deal. I was still in my cell when Pierpont and Boobie Clark split open his skull with a gun-butt busting me out. I'm almost as much a whiz at getting arrested as I am at avoiding it.

Crown Point was no crackerbox, I can tell you that. It took up a city block and was built better than most prisons. And the sheriff, Lillian Holley, wasn't the creampuff the press made her out to be, based on her sex, after I crashed out. She'd stepped into the office after the former sheriff, her husband, was shot to death by some screwball, and she didn't waste any time. She took firearms training, learned to pick ants off a hill with a chopper, and looked me square in the eye when they brought me in wearing bracelets: Public Enemy Number One face-to-face with Molly McGee. She was a tall woman, dressed like the president of a ladies' garden club, and brought sandwiches and beer for the gang of laws crowded around to make sure they got the credit they thought they had coming to them; but for me all she brought was that steely-eyed stare. Not in a million years would she have let her picture be taken with my arm on her shoulder, like that dope of a prosecutor. That was the finish of him; the press came down on him like a flock of crows.

But it wasn't the finish of me.

They said I carved a wooden gun and bluffed my way out of that hole. Well, it was a fake, sure enough, but it wasn't all wood, and I'm nobody's idea of an artist with a jack knife even if it was. The barrel was bored out with a drill press by Mr. None-of-Your-Business in Chicago, with the hollow handle of a safety razor slid in to make it look more genuine. You can get almost anything in jail if you're good to the turnkeys and you've got somebody on the outside; a decent imitation, if not a real gun. But it's part of the legend now. I gave it to my sister Audrey to hand down to her grandkids someday. See, I was a celebrity now, thanks to the press I got in stir. I scooped Stalin's purge.

That toy gun got me through a dozen doors. I don't know how many times I marched the length of that building, forward and back, collecting hostages and information on the layout, the number of armed men outside, and whether I could get to the garage without stepping into the open. At the end I had to cross through an exposed courtyard, every nerve standing on edge, in a scrum of hostages. I guess they were just as agitated as I was.

I smashed the carburetors in all the vehicles that could chase me and hopped into a sweet black Ford V-8 sedan, which was always my automobile of choice when I was working. It turned out to belong to Sheriff Holley. She took heat for that along with everything else.

Then I made the mistake of my life: Regret Number Six, if you're keeping count.

I drove a stolen car across the Indiana state line into Illinois. That made me a federal case. Before that, J. Edgar Hoover, that sawed-off little fairy, couldn't touch me. They're talking about making bank-robbing federal now, which is something else you can thank me for; but not then.

So now I was number one on the G-men's hit parade. It meant there was no place in the United States I could hole up safely for more than a few days.

Everyone knows about Little Bohemia. It was supposed to be a vacation for me and the boys and girls, a quiet lodge in the woods in Wisconsin, and it would have ended peaceful if the mom-and-pop that owned it didn't rat us out to the locals. All it came to was their house shot to pieces, a bunch of drunken fishermen with it, and Nelson two more notches on his belt. That made three feds for him; so far nobody's matched his record.

We had to leave the girls behind, but all of us desperate characters crawled out second-story windows and ran away through the woods like a herd of deer.

I went to cover after that, holing up in Chicago with a new face and a new girl. I can't be without a woman: Call it my weakness if you like, but I can never get such tender mercy from anyone else in this world. Polly's good company, though she's no Billie. She thinks I'm a salesman named Jimmy.

St. Paul will probably cost me double, given the present situation; that city understands the basic principles of supply and demand. I may have to go on the cuff until I make the score. But I need the contacts if I'm going to round up a crew I can count on.

Tonight, though, I'm taking Polly to the Biograph Theater, to see Clark Gable's latest. Her friend Anna's coming along, a third wheel if ever there was one, who wears red dresses that don't do a thing for her substantial figure; but who'd look for the world's most wanted fugitive between two women, one of them dressed for the circus? Tomorrow I'll take the train. If I make all the hook-ups I need, I'll boost a car and scout out some prospects on the way back.

Don't try to talk me out of it, America. You owe me.

—*John Dillinger*
*July 22, 1934*

# A Web of Books

*The three stories I've published so far involving Avery Sharecross comprise my clandestine series, never mentioned among my several others. Somehow, I think the dusty old bookseller's modesty would approve. He lets me revisit one of my great loves, the world of books; a web that snared me long ago. [Spoiler alert: Don't read this story until you've read "The Tree on Execution Hill."]*

The visitor stepped inside the bookshop and blinked. The muted light and cool, dank air seemed otherworldly after the bright heat of the New Mexico street. As he closed the door, feathers of dust clinging to the spines of the decaying volumes on the shelves crawled and twitched in the current of air. The place smelled of must.

"Can I help you?" bleated the old man seated behind the dented desk. He was thin and angular, his shoulders falling away under a fraying sweater. Dull black hair spilled untidily over his collar. His face was narrow and puckered and dominated by spectacles so thick he seemed to be peering from the other side of a fish tank.

"Are you the owner?"

The old man nodded. "My name is Sharecross."

"Jed Kirby. I'm an investigator with Southwestern Life and Property." He didn't offer to shake hands. The missing finger on his right hand—he'd tired of saying *souvenir of Vietnam*—provoked unwanted questions. "I tried to call you yesterday."

"The lines are down east of town. A Santa Ana blew through over the weekend."

Kirby dismissed this with a wave of his good hand.

"I'm looking for a man named Murchison, Alan Murchison. We think he has information about an item of missing property insured by us."

"I don't know the name. Is it a book that's missing?"

"A very rare volume titled *The Midnight Sky*, by James Edward Long, published in Edinburgh, Scotland, in 1758. About ten inches by seven, four hundred and fifty pages, bound in brown Morocco with gold leaf on the page ends. It was stolen from a private library in Albuquerque last month. We think Murchison is the thief."

The bookseller opened an enormous volume on his old gray desk, paged through it, read. "Yes. Only two copies are known to exist. Each is worth as much as some whole collections. What makes you think he'd come here?"

"He's on the run. He was nearly apprehended in Silver City, but he managed to elude the police. He'll probably try to unload the book for whatever he can get and use part of the money to skip to South America. Our information has him heading this way."

"Dear me, that seems like a lot of trouble over one book, even that one."

"The book's just part of it, although it's the part that most directly concerns us. The law would dearly love to have him. He murdered the owner in order to gain possession."

"Dear me."

"It pieces together like this." Kirby caught himself gesturing with the incomplete hand and switched. "Murchison, a dealer who supplies rare curiosities to collectors who don't ask questions, went to this man Scullock with an offer to buy the book. When Scullock refused to sell, Murchison lost control and split the fellow's cranium with a bronze bust of Homer the police found near the body. Then he grabbed the book and left. When the customer he had lined up got suspicious and backed out of the deal, he took off."

Sharecross's forehead stacked with deep wrinkles. "Your company must be particularly anxious to recover the item, since you beat the police here."

"It's insured for two hundred thousand dollars, payable to Scullock's heirs if we fail to get it back. MY employers aren't in the business for their health."

"Who is?" The old man stretched a scrawny arm and lifted a book the size and thickness of a bathroom tile from a stack at his feet. "Two hundred thousand is far outside my budget, Mr. Kirby. This is more my speed." He handed it to the visitor.

It was bound in burgundy leather, and heavier than it looked. Kirby ran fingers over the hand-tooling, opened it carefully, and glanced at the publisher's ads bound into the back of the book. "First edition?"

"Third. Browning's *Ring and the Book*, the one with the erratum on page sixty-seven. I paid seven-fifty for it in Las Cruces two years ago. That's more than I can afford to pay for any book, but I couldn't resist it. The pension I get from the Santa Fe Police Department won't stand that kind of strain often."

Kirby looked up, startled. "You were a policeman?"

"Detective. Many years ago, I'm afraid."

Too many, thought the other. He'd probably retired before two-way radios. Kirby returned the volume. "Old books don't really interest me. You'd know Murchison if you saw him. He's small, kind of fragile-looking, with prematurely white hair. Wears tweed jackets and smokes a pipe."

A fresh furrow joined the others on Sharecross's brow. The other spotted it. "He's been in, hasn't he?"

"A man answering that description, yesterday." He looked down at the Browning distractedly. "But it was to buy a book, not sell one. A badly dilapidated copy of Shakespeare's tragedies for ten dollars; I thought it overpriced at that, but he didn't haggle. He said his name was Thacker. I think he's staying at the hotel; or he was."

"Where's that?"

"Across the street, next to the town well."

Kirby hurried out. As the door closed behind him, he glimpsed Sharecross easing another heavy tome down from a high shelf.

Twenty minutes later the visitor was back. Behind the desk, the bookseller lifted his eyebrows at him over the big book. *The*

*Directory of Book Collectors*, it said on the spine. A subtitle said it was the current year's edition.

"What kind of law you got around here?" Kirby demanded.

Sharecross hesitated. "Sheriff McCreedy. But he's at the county seat. There's no way to reach him with the telephone lines down, short of driving twenty miles. What's wrong?"

"Murchison's dead. Someone shot him."

"Shot him! Are you sure?"

"Bullets make holes. The blood's still fresh." Kirby paused. "The book isn't in his room. I searched. His door was unlocked."

Sharecross dragged over the old-fashioned upright telephone on his desk.

"You said the lines were down," Kirby said.

"Not in town. Hello, Birdie?" He spoke into the mouthpiece. "Birdie, get hold of Uncle Ned and ask him to fetch the sheriff. It's urgent." He rang off. To Kirby:

"Ned Scoffield's pushing a hundred, but he drives that old Indian motorcycle of his like Evel Knievel. He'll have the law here by sundown."

"Whoever killed Murchison was after the book. Now that he has it, there's no way he'll be within fifty miles of here by sundown."

"Maybe he doesn't have it. Did you search Murchison's car?"

"Car!" He cuffed his forehead. "Stupid! He didn't walk here. Where would I find it?"

"Behind the hotel would be my guess. It's where all the guests park. Maybe you should wait for the sheriff."

But the old man was talking to the visitor's back. He was already out the door.


Kirby got the dead man's license number from an upset clerk at the front desk. The plate belonged to a late-model sedan under a skin of desert dust. The inside was an oven. He stripped off his jacket and got to work. After half an hour he climbed out, empty-handed and gasping, and leaned back against a fender to mop his face with a soaked handkerchief. Sharecross approached through shimmering waves of heat, his hefty directory under one arm.

"Nothing?"

Kirby shook his head. He was too overheated to talk.

"I see you checked out the trunk and engine compartment." The bookseller nodded at the open lid and dislodged hood. "I just came from Murchison's room. He was shot twice at close range. Whoever did it must have used a silencer or he'd have alerted everyone in the hotel."

"What were you doing there?" Kirby was cooling off slowly. Dusk was gathering.

"I conducted a search of my own. Once a cop, always a cop. There's something missing besides *The Midnight Sky*."

"A towel?"

"The Shakespeare I sold him. You didn't happen to find it?"

"No, but why should you care? You got your ten bucks."

"It seemed strange that a thief who'd kill for James Edward Long's magnum opus would bother with so common an item. Also, I asked some of the other merchants what they could tell me about Thacker, or Murchison, or whatever he was calling himself. Carl Lathrop at the dry goods said he sold Thacker thirty feet of extension cord last night, just before closing."

"Why extension cord, of all things?"

"We may never find out. Every investigation has a loose end, usually more than one. I'd rather concentrate on why was he wasting time here when he knew the law and your company were hard on his heels. Why stop here at all, for that matter? Why not head straight for old Mexico and peddle the book in Acapulco or Cancun, where the wealthy tourists congregate? That's a lot of mistakes for an experienced criminal."

"He'd never been chased before. Maybe he panicked."

"The panicked usually run."

"Paralyzed with fear, then."

"Maybe. Or maybe he came here to meet someone."

"A dame, in this town? From what I've seen, the entire female population dated Methuselah."

"I was thinking an accomplice. Maybe he wasn't in this alone. When the deal with the customer fell through, the partner decided to eliminate Murchison, sell the book for whatever he could get, and keep the money for himself; or maybe it was Murchison who got greedy, but it didn't go down the way he had planned. I was thirty years with Homicide, and in all that time I never came across one example of honor among thieves."

"You were with Homicide?"

"I was in command." Sharecross polished his glasses on the sleeve of his old sweater. His eyes, sardine-colored behind the lenses, were as sharp as flint. "Well," he said, putting the glasses back on, "we can stand here spinning theories all night and freeze to death. The desert cools off fast when the sun goes down. Why don't we go back to the shop and wait for the sheriff?"

On the way they passed the town well. It was partially boarded over and the ancient peaked roof leaned ten degrees off plumb.

"If it's dry it should be torn down and the hole filled in," Kirby said. "It's a safety hazard. Someone could fall in."

"You're probably right, but I'll be sorry to see it go. When it does I'll be the second-oldest thing in town after Uncle Ned Scoffield."

The bookshop seemed absolutely gloomy by electric light. Pacing up and down the aisles, glancing at the titles on the shelves, Kirby asked his host why he quit the police. "Job get too tough?"

"It got too easy. The pattern never varies. Someone kills someone else, then tries to confuse the issue. But the more he tries, the simpler the case gets. In the end he catches himself in the web he spun. Tracing the provenance of a book, now; that's a challenge."

Sirens shattered the desert peace. Two blue and white prowl cars ground to a halt in front of the shop, their lights throbbing and splashing red and blue all over the street. A middle-aged man whose tanned face matched the color of his uniform shirt strode into the shop, towing three deputies in similar dress. They all wore Stetsons and high boots.

"What's going on, Avery?" demanded the middle-aged man.

"Murder, Sheriff. The victim is registered at the hotel under the name Thacker, though he's known elsewhere as Alan Murchison. You'll find him in room fourteen with two bullets in his chest."

He inclined his head toward Kirby.

"I think a paraffin test of this gentleman's hands will show within a reasonable margin of certainty that he fired the gun."

Before Kirby could react, one of the deputies seized him and hurled him up against a wall full of books. He was forced to brace himself on his arms and spread his feet.

"The old man's crazy!" he shouted. "Why would I—" Rough hands frisked him.

Sharecross said, "You won't find the gun on him. My guess is he chucked it in the well. As things stood, he barely had time to kill Murchison, search his room for the book, ditch the murder weapon, and come back here to report the crime."

Sheriff McCreedy told his deputies to watch the prisoner and accompanied Sharecross outside, at his invitation. The sun was almost gone.

"I've something else to show you before we look at the body." The old man gave him the particulars as they walked.

"The man you arrested was the dead man's partner," he said, when he finished bringing the sheriff up to date. "I should refer to him as Jed Carlisle instead of Kirby. That's the name he's listed under in *The Directory of Book Collectors*. Carlisle was the customer who commissioned Murchison to find *The Midnight Sky*. The way

I read things, Murchison tried to shake him down for more money by threatening to pin the owner's murder on the customer; which was almost certainly the case. Carlisle agreed to his terms, said he'd meet him here. It's an out-of-the-way place, perfect for what he had in mind: It's just a speck on the map, after all. Then he came here, posing as an insurance investigator to throw off the authorities, and shot Murchison to death.

"He made three mistakes," Sharecross continued. "The first was failing to find out where the book was hidden before he silenced his victim."

"But where—?"

They'd stopped in the middle of the street. "Bear with me a little longer. I don't think Kirby, or Carlisle, has much respect for rural law officers, Sheriff. When he failed to find the book in the hotel room or in Murchison's car, he was content to sit back and let you comb the town for it, confident that when it was found he could step forward and claim it for his 'company.' I'm sure when you search him you'll find business cards and all kinds of credentials that would pass muster with the kind of dopes he expected to find in charge of the investigation."

McCreedy smiled. "I always like that part. Being underestimated by crooks is what got me elected, on my arrest record."

"I told him straight out it's the ones who think they're clever that are easiest to nail. I always tried to play fair with the enemy. That's what got me promoted, on *my* arrest record."

"Did you remind him of the name of this town?"

"Good Advice? That would be stating the obvious."

"What made you suspect him in the first place?"

"He seemed to have more than a layman's knowledge of that book. I tested him by handing him a rare Browning. He claimed that kind of thing didn't interest him; if that were so he'd simply have glanced at it to be polite and handed it back. Instead he stroked the binding, lifted open the cover as if it were made of glass, looked closely at the advertisements bound at the back. That's what I do, every time. I doubt he could help himself any more than I could. Old habits." He shrugged. "After that I consulted an odd little source, valuable for the kind of gossipy minutiae you won't find in *Who's Who in Book Collecting*. Most booksellers won't bother with it, but I'm something of a vacuum cleaner for texts on my vocation. I went through it entry by entry until I found one that fit the man I knew as Jed Kirby. There aren't very many wealthy bibliophiles missing the third finger from their right hand. He cut it badly slitting open uncut pages with a paper knife and it had to be amputated. I understand he was more upset about having stained a rare book with his blood than the loss of the digit; that's typical."

"You said he made *three* mistakes. What was the third?"

"Look in the well."

They were standing beside the ancient excavation. Shadows filled it. McCreedy unhooked his flash from his belt and trained the beam down inside.

"No, look under the roof."

He redirected the beam. The rod that had once supported the bucket now supported something that looked nearly as old as the well itself: a thick volume of paper bound in crumbling leather, the covers split alongside the hinge of the spine, secured to the rod with a black knot.

"So that's *The Midnight Sky*," the sheriff said. "It doesn't look like much."

"That's because it isn't." Sharecross jerked loose the knot. The book dropped into the well, vanishing into the shadows. As it did, an oil-skin-wrapped parcel rose into the glare of the flashlight.

The bookseller caught the package before it reached the rod, untied it, looping its former tether around the rod, and undid the wrapping. Handsome leather and bright gold leaf glittered as if with an illumination of their own.

"Carlisle's third mistake, Sheriff. He was in too much of a hurry when he disposed of the gun in the well. It might have occurred to him he wasn't the first who thought it an ideal hiding place. Tied securely, the Shakespeare kept *The Midnight Sky* accessible; being almost the same size and weight as the more valuable book, it made the ideal counterweight. Note what Murchison tied them with."

The sheriff stared at the black thing looped around the rod. "Looks like ordinary extension cord."

"Thirty feet long would be my guess. If he'd bought that much rope and Carlisle found out, the well would have seemed the logical next step. Electrical cord was just offbeat enough to throw anyone off."

"Except you."

"It was a guess. So were Murchison's motives. He probably rigged this to buy time while he found a way to double-cross Carlisle, probably the same way he was double-crossed himself. I told Carlisle there was no honor among thieves."

He shook his head sadly.

"A web of books, spun from leather and buckram and paper. Murchison used a book to help conceal the book he'd committed murder to obtain. That book, and Carlisle's obsession to have it, drove him to murder the murderer, before the murderer could murder him. A book made me suspect him, and another book led to his identification and apprehension. And now, Sheriff"—he paused uncomfortably and adjusted the spectacles on the thin nose—"I imagine it's your intention to, er, throw the book at him."

Sheriff McCreedy stared at him in mute accusation.

"Yes. Well." Sharecross turned back in the direction of the bookshop.

# State of Grace

*This is the only lighthearted story in the collection. When I was asked to write a story for a private eye anthology, I'd just finished an Amos Walker novel and needed a break from the character. Ralph Poteet is the flip side of the coin: a sleazy grifter who will do almost anything for a hundred dollars. His more lovable qualities include dimness of intellect and phenomenally bad luck. I got one complaint claiming I'd maligned the Catholic Church (which was not my intention), but I felt vindicated when the pedophilia scandal broke. As of this writing, the Vatican is making a saint out of the pope who presided over the cover-up.*

"Ralph? This is Lyla."

"Who the hell is Lyla?"

"Lyla Dane. I live in the apartment above you, for chrissake. You ask me for a freebie almost every day."

"The hooker." He'd never asked her name.

"You live over a dirty bookstore. What do you want for a neighbor, a fucking rocket scientist?"

Ralph Poteet sat up in bed and rumpled his mouse-colored hair. His scalp felt like grout. He fumbled the alarm clock off the night table and held it very close to his good eye. He laid it face-down and scowled at the receiver in his hand. "It's two-thirty ayem."

"Thanks. My watch stopped and I knew if I called you you'd tell me what time it is. Listen, you're like a cop, right?"

"Not at two-thirty ayem."

"I'll give you a hundred dollars to come up here now."

He blew his nose on the sheet. "Ain't that supposed to go the other way around?"

"You coming up or not? You're not the only dick in town. I just called you because you're handy."

He resisted the temptation to ask her just how many dicks there were in town.

"What's the squeal?"

"I got a dead priest in my bed."

He said he was on his way and hung up. A square gin bottle slid off the blanket. He caught it before it hit the floor, but it was empty and he dropped it. He put on his Tyrolean hat with a feather in the band, found his pants on the floor half under the bed, and pulled

68

them on over his pajamas. He stuck bare feet into his loafers and because it was October he pulled on his sportcoat, grunting with the effort. He was forty-three years old and forty pounds overweight. He looked for his gun just because it was 2:30 A.M., couldn't find it, and went out.

Lyla Dane was just five feet and ninety pounds in a pink kimono and slippers with carnations on the toes. She wore her black hair in a pageboy like Anna May Wong, but the Oriental effect fell short of her round Occidental face. "You look like crap," she told Ralph at the door.

"You look like the girl on the dashboard of a '57 Chevy. Where's the hundred?"

"Don't you want to see the stiff first?"

"What do I look like, a pervert?"

"You could be the poster boy." She opened a drawer in the telephone stand and counted a hundred in twenties and tens into his palm.

He stuck the money in a pocket and followed her through a small living room decorated by K-Mart into a smaller bedroom containing a Queen Anne bed that had cost twice as much as all the other furniture combined and took up most of the space in the room.

The rest of the space was taken up by Monsignor John Breame, pastor of Our Lady of the Agonies, a cathedral Ralph sometimes used to exchange pictures for money, although not so much lately because the divorce business was on the slide; No-Fault was killing the P.I. trade. He recognized the Monsignor's pontifical belly under the flesh-colored satin sheet: Cheez Whiz on the Communion wafers wasn't such a good idea. The Monsignor's face was purple.

"He a regular?" Ralph found a Diamond matchstick in a pocket and stuck it between his teeth.

"Couple of times a month. Tonight I thought he was breathing a little hard after. Then he wasn't."

"Try CPR?"

"I don't kiss johns on the mouth. It's a personal principle." She lit a joint.

He took a hit off the secondhand. "What do you want me to do?"

"Spray-paint him gold and set him up in the living room as a holy icon. What do you think? Get rid of him. Cops find him here the Christers'll run me out of town on a cross. I got a business to maintain."

"Cost you another hundred."

"I just gave you a hundred."

"That was for coming up here. You're lucky I don't charge by the pound. Look at that gut."

"You look at it. He liked the missionary position."

"What else would he?"

She drew in smoke, held it, let it stutter out, then got the hundred and gave it to him. He stuck it in another pocket. He kept a meticulous filing system. The rest of his life was chaos to the point of apocalyptic.

"Scram," he said.

"Where to?"

"There's beds all over town. You probably been in half of 'em. Or go find an all-night movie if you don't feel like working. I think *Hung 'Em High*'s still playing at the Tomcat on Eight Mile. Just don't come back before dawn. It'll take me at least that long to get this tub of lard down six flights of stairs."

He crossed himself. He'd been an altar boy until Father Emmanuel caught him shooting craps behind the rectory.

She dressed and started toward the door, then went back and emptied the money drawer into her shoulder bag. Ralph, disappointed, consoled himself by spearing his toothpick through the roach she'd left smoldering in a tin tray and taking a toke; it was better than he could afford. Then he looked up a number in the city directory and called it from the telephone in the living room. A voice like ground glass answered.

"Bishop Stoneman?" Ralph asked.

"It's three ayem."

"Thank you. My name is Ralph Poteet. I'm a private detective. I'm sorry to have to inform you Monsignor Breame is dead."

"Mary Mother of God! In bed?"

He was in the middle of a hit. He smothered a giggle. "Yeah."

"Was he—do you know if he was in a state of grace?"

"That's what I wanted to talk to you about," Ralph said.

The man Bishop Stoneman sent was tall and gaunt, with a complexion like wet pulp and colorless hair cropped down to stubble. He had on a black coat buttoned to the neck and looked like an early martyr. He said his name was Morgan.

Together they wrapped the Monsignor in the soiled bedding and carried him down six flights of stairs, stopping a dozen times to rest, then laid him on the back seat of a big Buick Electra parked between streetlamps. Ralph stood guard at the car while Morgan went back up for the Monsignor's clothes. It was nearly 4:00 A.M. and their only witness was a scrawny cat who lost interest after a few minutes and stuck one leg up in the air to lick its balls.

Ralph said, "If a man could do that, Lyla'd be out of business."

Morgan threw the bundle of clothing into the front seat and handed Ralph an envelope containing three hundred dollars in fifties. He said he'd handle things from there. Ralph watched him drive off and went back up to bed. He slept the sleep of the innocent, or at least of the well-set-up; he'd made five hundred dollars in one night. A piano player in a first-rate lounge couldn't do better than that.

He woke up to the sound of fire sirens grinding down in front of his building. He hadn't even heard the explosion in Lyla Dane's apartment, directly above his own.

"Go away."

"That's no way to talk to your partner," Ralph said.

"Ex-partner. You got the boot and I did, too. Now I'm giving it to you. Scram. Skedaddle. Take it on the ankles, and please let the door hit you on the ass on your way out."

Dale English was a special investigator with the sheriff's department who kept his office in the City-County Building, since renamed for a deceased former mayor, beloved and corrupt. Dale had a monolithic face and fierce black eyebrows like Lincoln's, creating an effect he tried to soften with pink shirts and knobby knitted ties. He and Ralph had shared a city prowl car for two years, until some evidence went missing from the property room. Both had been dismissed, English without prejudice because none of the incriminating items had been found in his possession; unlike the case with Ralph. The department was still buzzing with just how a man with no knowledge of geometry had managed to cram a fifty-seven-piece set of Dresden china into his locker in the basement of police headquarters.

"The boot didn't hurt you none," Ralph said.

"No, it just cost me my wife and my kid and seven years' seniority. I'd be a lieutenant now."

"Who needs the ulcers?" Ralph lowered his bulk onto the vinyl-and-aluminum chair in front of English's desk. "I wouldn't hang this on you if I could go to the city cops. Someone's out to kill me."

"Only one? Tell him I said good luck."

"I ain't kidding."

"Am I smiling?"

"You know that hooker that got blown up this morning?"

"The gas explosion? I read about it."

"Yeah, well, it wasn't no accident. I'm betting the arson boys find a circuit breaker in the wall switch. You know what that means."

"Sure. Somebody lets himself in and turns on the gas on the stove and puts a breaker in the switch so when the guy comes home the spark blows him to hell. What was the hooker into and what was your angle?"

"It's more like who was into the hooker." Ralph told him the rest.

"This the same Monsignor Breame was found by a novice, counting angels in his bed at Our Lady of the Agonies rectory this morning?"

"Thanks to me and this bug Morgan."

"So what do you want?"

"Hell, protection. The blowup was meant for me. Morgan thought I'd be going back to that same apartment and set it up while I was waiting for him to come down with Breame's clothes."

"Bishops don't kill people over priests that can't keep their vows in their pants."

Ralph screwed up his good eye. Its mate looked like a sourball someone had spat out. "What world you living in, Dale? Shape the Church is in, he'd do just that to keep it quiet."

"Go away, Ralph."

"Well, pick up Morgan, at least. He can't be hard to find. He looks like one of those devout creeps you see skulking around paintings of the Crucifixion."

"Somebody's been hanging around the DIA. That where you're selling dirty pictures to your clients now, the art museum?"

"Hey, I'm giving you a lead."

"Go to the city cops. I don't have jurisdiction."

"That ain't why you won't do it. Hey, I told Internal Affairs you didn't have nothing to do with what went down in Property."

"It would've carried more weight if you'd submitted to a lie detector test. Mine was inconclusive."

He paged through a report on his desk without looking at it.

"I'll run the name Morgan and the description you gave me through the computer and see what it coughs up. Either there won't be anything or too much. A lot of guys look like Christopher Walken on the Atkins Diet, and Morgan's Number Three on the list of most popular AKAs."

"Thanks, buddy."

"You sure you didn't take pictures? It'd be your style to try and put the squeeze on a bishop."

"I thought about it, but my camera's in hock." Ralph got up. "You can get me at my place. They got the fire out before it reached my floor."

"Lucky you. Gin flames are tough to put out."

• • •

He was driving a brand-new red Riviera he'd promised to sell for a lawyer friend who was serving two years for suborning to commit perjury, only he hadn't gotten around to it yet. He parked in a handicapped zone near his building and climbed stairs smelling of smoke and firemen's rubber boots. Inside his apartment, which was also his office, he rewound the tape on his answering machine and played back a threatening call from a loan shark named Zwingman, a reminder from a dentist's receptionist with a NutraSweet voice that last month's root canal was still unpaid for, and a message from a heavy-breather that he had to play back three times before deciding it was a man. He was staring toward the door, his attention on the tape, when a square of white paper slithered over the threshold.

That day he was wearing his legal gun, a short-nosed .38 Colt, in a clip on his belt, and an orphan High Standard .22 Magnum derringer in an ankle holster that brought out his prickly heat. Drawing the Colt, he lunged and tore open the door, just in time to hear the street door closing below.

He swung around and crossed to the street window. Through it he saw a narrow figure in a long black coat and the back of a close-cropped head crossing against traffic. The man rounded the corner and vanished.

Ralph missed the holster the first time, stooped to pick it up, and retrieved the note with it. It was addressed to him in a round, shaped hand:

*Mr. Poteet:*
    *If it is not inconvenient, your presence at my home could prove to your advantage and mine.*

*Cordially,*
*Philip Stoneman,*
*Bishop-in-Ordinary*

Clipped to it was a hundred-dollar bill.

Bishop Stoneman lived in a refurbished brownstone in a neighborhood that the city had reclaimed from slum by evicting the residents and sandblasting graffiti off the buildings. The bell was answered by a youngish bald man in a dark suit and clerical collar, who introduced himself as Brother Edwards and directed Ralph to a curving staircase, then retired to be seen no more. Ralph didn't hear Morgan climbing behind him until something hard probed his right kidney. A hand patted him down and removed the Colt from its clip. "End of the hall."

The bishop was a tall old man, nearly as thin as Morgan, with iron-gray hair and a face that fell away to the white shackle of his collar. He rose from behind a redwood desk to greet his visitor in an old-fashioned black frock coat that made him look like a crow. The room was large and square and smelled of leather from the books on the built-in shelves and pipe tobacco. Morgan entered behind Ralph and closed the door.

"Thank you for coming, Mr. Poteet. Please sit down."

"Thank Ben Franklin." But he settled into a deep leather chair that gripped his buttocks like a big friendly hand in a soft glove.

"I'm grateful for the chance to thank you in person," Stoneman said, sitting in his big swivel. "I'm very disappointed in Monsignor Breame. I'd hoped he would take my place at the head of the diocese."

"Well, maybe he got head. You bucking for cardinal?"

Stoneman smiled.

"I suppose you've shown yourself worthy of confidence. Yes, His Holiness has offered me the red hat. The appointment will be announced next month at the Vatican."

"That why you tried to croak me?"

"Excuse me?"

"Whack me. Take me for a ride. Give me a one-way ticket to Box City." Ralph frowned, seeking the translation. "Make me a martyr: Ralph, patron saint of shamuses, keyhole-peepers, and knights of the infrared lens. Got a ring to it, don't it? I guess your heir apparent cashing in in a hooker's bed wouldn't look so good in Rome."

One corner of the desk supported a silver tray containing two long-stemmed glasses and a cut-crystal decanter half full of ruby-colored liquid. Stoneman removed the stopper and filled both glasses.

"This is an excellent Madeira, put down in 1936 during the Spanish Civil War. I confess that the austere life allows me two mild vices. The other is tobacco."

"What are we celebrating?" Ralph didn't pick up his glass.

"Your new appointment as chief of diocesan security. The position pays well and the hours are flexible. Some days you might even not need to show up."

"In return for which I forget about Monsignor Breame. Who's he again?" He grinned.

"And entrust all related material to me. You took pictures, of course." Stoneman sipped from his glass.

Ralph lifted his. "I'd be pretty stupid not to, considering what happened to Lyla Dane."

"I heard about that tragedy. That child's soul could have been saved."

"You should've thought about that before your boy Morgan croaked her." Ralph gulped off half his wine. It tasted bitter. Whatever the Spanish Civil War was, it should have bombed the vineyard.

The bishop laid a bony hand atop an ancient ornate Bible on the desk. It was as big as a cornerstone.

"This belonged to St. Thomas. More; not Aquinas. I have a weakness for religious antiques."

"I thought you only had two vices."

The air in the room stirred slightly. Ralph turned to see who had entered, but his vision was thickening. Morgan was a shimmering shadow. The glass dropped from Ralph's hand. He bent to retrieve it and came up with the derringer.

Stoneman's shout echoed. Ralph fired twice at the shadow and pitched headfirst into its depths.

He awoke feeling pretty much the way he did most mornings, with his head throbbing and his stomach turning over. He wanted to turn over with it, but he was stretched out on a hard, flat surface with his ankles strapped down and his arms tied above his head. He was looking up at water-stained tile. His joints ached.

"The sedative was in the glass's hollow stem," Stoneman was saying. "You've been out for two hours. The unpleasant effect is temporary, rather like a hangover."

"I had worse." Ralph's tongue moved sluggishly. "Did I get the son of a bitch?"

"No, you missed rather badly. It required persuasion to get Morgan to carry you down here to the basement instead of killing you on the spot. He was quite upset."

"Tell him I'll try to do better next time." Ralph squirmed. There was something familiar about the position he was tied in. For some reason he thought of Mrs. Thornton, his ninth-grade American Lit. teacher. *What is the significance of Poe's "Pit and the Pendulum" to the transcendentalist movement?*

His organs shriveled.

"Another antique," said the bishop. "The Inquisition did not end when General Lasalle entered Madrid, but went on for several years in the provinces. This particular rack was still in use after Torquemada's death. The gears are original. The wheel is new, and of course I had to replace the ropes. Morgan?"

A shoe scraped the floor and a spoked shadow fluttered across Ralph's vision. His arms tightened. He gasped.

"That's enough. We don't want to put Mr. Poteet back under." To Ralph: "Morgan just returned from your apartment. He found neither pictures nor film nor even a camera. Where are they?"

"I was lying. I didn't take no pictures."

"Morgan."

Ralph shrieked.

"Enough!" Stoneman's fallen-away face moved into Ralph's vision. His eyes were fanatic. "A few more turns will sever your spine. You could be spoon-fed for the rest of your life. Do you think that after failing to kill you in that apartment I would hesitate to cripple you? Where are the pictures?"

"I didn't take none!"

"Morgan!"

"*No!*"

It ended in a howl. His armpits were on fire. The ropes creaked.

The bishop's face jerked away. The spoked shadow fluttered. The tension went out of Ralph's arms suddenly, and relief poured into his joints. A shot flattened the air. Two more answered it. Something struck the bench Ralph was lying on and drove a splinter into his back. He thought at first he'd been shot, but the pain was nothing; he'd just been through worse. He squirmed onto his hip and saw Morgan, one black-clad arm stained and glistening, leveling a heavy automatic at a target behind Ralph's back. Scrambling out of the line of fire, Ralph jerked his bound hands and the rack's wheel, six feet in diameter with handles bristling from it as from a ship's helm, spun around. One of the handles slapped the gun from Morgan's hand. Something cracked past Ralph's left ear and Morgan fell back against the tile wall and slid down it. The shooting stopped.

Ralph wriggled onto his other hip. A man he didn't know, in a houndstooth coat with a revolver in his hand, had Bishop Stoneman spread-eagled against a wall and was groping in his robes for weapons. Dale English came off the stairs with the Ruger he'd carried since Ralph was his partner. He bent over Morgan on the floor, then straightened and holstered the gun. He looked at Ralph. "I guess you're okay."

"I am if you got a pocketknife."

"Arson boys found the circuit breaker in the wall switch just like you said." He cut Ralph's arms free and sawed through the straps on his ankles. "When you didn't answer your phone I went to your place and found Stoneman's note."

"He confessed to the hooker's murder."

"I know. I heard him."

"How the hell long were you listening?"

"We had to have enough to pin him to it, didn't we?"

"You son of a bitch. You just wanted to hear me holler."

"Couldn't help it. You sure got lungs."

"We even now?"

"We'll never be even. But we're closer."

"I got to go to the toilet."

"Stick around after," English said. "I need a statement to hand to the City boys. They won't like County sticking its face in this."

Ralph hobbled upstairs. When he was through in the bathroom he found his hat and coat and headed out. At the front door he turned around and went back into the bishop's study, where he hoisted St. Thomas More's Bible under one arm. He knew a bookseller who would probably give him a hundred bucks for it.

# The Used

*I was impressed with how well this one held up after more than thirty years. It was the first story I sold to Cathleen Jordan after she became editor-in-chief of* Alfred Hitchcock's Mystery Magazine; *before that, she'd been my editor at Doubleday. Sadly, this great lady is no longer with us. But apart from the satisfaction of the sale, I had the bonus of meeting John Lutz, whose fine story "Time Exposure" appeared in the same issue, and beginning a friendship that has lasted to this day.*

"But I never been to Iowa!" Murch said.

His visitor sighed. "Of course not. No one has. That's why we're sending you there."

Slouched in the worn leather armchair in the office Murch kept at home, Adamson looked more like a high school basketball player than a federal agent. He had baby-fat features without a breath of whisker and collar-length sandy hair and wore faded Levi's with a tweed jacket too short in the sleeves and a paisley tie at three-quarter mast. His voice was changing, for God's sake. The slight bulge under his left arm might have been a sandwich from home.

Murch paced, coming to a stop at the basement window. His lawn needed mowing. The thought of it awakened the bursitis in his right shoulder. "What'll I do there? Don't they raise wheat or something like that? What's a wheat farmer need with a bookkeeper?"

"You won't be a bookkeeper. I explained all this before." The agent sat up, resting his forearms on his bony knees. "In return for your testimony regarding illegal contributions made by your employer to the campaigns of Congressmen Disdale and Reicher and Senator Van Horn, the Justice Department promises immunity from prosecution. You will also be provided with protection during the trial, and afterwards a new identity and relocation to Iowa. When you get there, you'll find a job waiting for you selling hardware, courtesy of your Uncle Sam."

"What do I know about hardware? My business is with numbers."

"An accounting position seemed inadvisable, on the off chance Redman's people traced you west. They'd never think of looking for you behind a sales counter."

Murch swung around. "You said he wouldn't be able to trace me!"

Adamson's lips pursed, lending him the appearance of a teenage Cupid. "I won't lie and say it hasn't happened. But in those cases there were big syndicate operations involved, with plenty of capital to spend. Jules Redman is light cargo by comparison. It's the senator and the congressmen we want, but we have to knock him down to get to them."

"What's the matter, they turn you down?"

The agent looked at him blankly.

Murch had to smile.

"Come on, I ain't been in this line eighteen years I don't see how it jerks. Maybe these guys been giving your agency a hard time on appropriations or—" He broke off, his face brightening further. "Say, didn't I read where this Van Horn is asking for an investigation into clandestine operations? Yeah, and maybe the others support him. So you sniff around till something stinks and then tell them if they play ball you'll scratch sand over it. Only they don't feel like playing, so now you go for the jugular. Am I close?"

"I'm just a field operative, Mr. Murch. I leave politics to politicians." But the grudging respect in the agent's tone was enlightening.

"What happens if I decide not to testify?"

"Then you'll be wearing those numbers you're so good at on your shirt. For three counts of conspiracy to bribe a member of the United States Congress."

They were watching each other when the doorbell rang upstairs. Murch jumped.

"That'll be your escort," Adamson suggested. "I've arranged for a room at a motel in the suburbs. The local police are lending a couple of plainclothesmen to stay there with you until the trial Monday. It's up to you whether I ask them to take you to jail instead."

"One room?" The bookkeeper's lip curled.

"There's an economy move on in Washington." Adamson got out of the chair and stood waiting. The doorbell sounded again.

"I want a color TV in the room," said Murch. "Tell your boss no color TV, no deal."

The agent didn't smile. "I'll tell him." He went up to answer the door.

He shared a frame bungalow at the motel between the railroad and the river with a detective sergeant named Kirdy and his relief, a lean, chinless officer who watched football all day with the sound turned down. He held a transistor radio in his lap; it was tuned to the races. Kirdy looked smaller than he was. Though his head barely reached the bridge of Murch's nose, he took a size forty-six jacket and had to turn sideways to clear his shoulders through doorways. He had kind eyes set incongruously in a slab of granite. No-Chin never spoke except to warn his charge away from windows. Kirdy's conversation centered around his granddaughter, a blond tyke of whom he had a wallet full of photos. The bathroom was heated only intermittently by an electric baseboard unit and the building shuddered whenever a train went past. But Murch had his color TV.

At half past ten Monday morning, he was escorted into court by Adamson and another agent who looked like a rock musician. Jules Redman sat at the defense table with his attorney. Murch's employer was small and dark, with an old-time bullfighter's handlebar moustache and glossy black hair combed over a bald spot. Their gazes met while the bookkeeper was being sworn in, and from then until recess was called at noon, Redman's tan eyes remained on the man in the witness chair.

Charles Anthony Murch—his full name felt strange on his tongue when the court officer asked him for it—was on the stand two days. His testimony was complicated, having to do with dates and transactions made through dummy corporations, and he consulted his notebook often while the jurors stifled yawns and the spectators fidgeted and inspected their fingernails. After adjournment the first day, the witness was whisked along a circuitous route to a hotel near the airport, where Kirdy and his partner awaited their duty. On the way, Adamson was talkative and in good spirits. Already he spoke of how his agency would proceed against the congressmen and Senator Van Horn after Redman was convicted. Murch was silent, remembering his employer's eyes.

The defense attorney, white-haired and grandfatherly behind a pair of half-glasses, kept his seat during cross-examination the next morning, reading from a computer printout sheet on the table in front of him while the government's case slowly fell to pieces. Murch had thought that his dismissal from that contracting firm upstate was off the books, and he was surprised to learn that someone had penetrated his double-entry system at the insurance company he had left in Chicago. Based on this record, the lawyer accused the witness of entering the so-called campaign donations into Redman's ledger to cover his own thefts. The jurors' faces were unreadable, but as the imputation continued, Murch saw the corners of the defendant's moustache rise slightly and watched Adamson's eyes growing dull.

The jury was out twenty-two hours, a state record for that kind of case. Jules Redman was found guilty of resisting arrest, reduced from assaulting a police officer (he'd lost his temper and knocked down a detective during an unsuccessful search of his office for evidence), and was acquitted on three counts of bribery. He was sentenced to time served and fined five thousand dollars.

Adamson was out the door on the reporters' scurrying heels. Murch hurried to catch up.

"You don't live right, Charlie."

The bookkeeper held up at the hoarse comment. Redman's diminutive frame slid past him in the aisle and was swallowed up by a crowd of well-wishers gathered near the door.

The agent kept a twelve-by-ten cubicle in the federal building two floors up from the courtroom where Redman had been set free. When Murch burst in, Adamson was slumped behind a gray steel desk deep in conversation with his rock-musician partner.

"We *had* a deal," corrected the agent, after Murch's panicky interruption. His colleague stood by brushing his long hair out of his eyes. "It was made in good faith. We gave you a chance to volunteer any information from your past that might put our case in jeopardy. You didn't take advantage of it, and now we're all treading water in the toilet."

"How was I to know they was gonna dig up that stuff about those other two jobs? *You* investigated me. You didn't find nothing." The ex-witness's hands made wet marks on the desk top.

"Our methods aren't Redman's. It takes longer to subpoena personnel files than it does to screw a Magnum into a clerk's ear and say gimme. Now I know why he didn't try to take you out before the trial." He paused. "Is there anything else?"

"Damn right there's something else! You promised me Iowa, win or lose."

Adamson reached inside his jacket and extracted a long narrow envelope like the airlines used to put tickets in. Murch's heart leaped. He was reaching for the envelope when the agent tore it in half. He put the pieces together and tore them. Again, and then he let the bits flutter to the desk.

For a numb moment the bookkeeper goggled at the scraps. Then he lunged, grasping Adamson's lapels in both hands and lifting. "Redman's a killer!" He shook him. The agent clawed at his wrists, but Murch's fingers were strong from years cramped around pencils and the handles of adding machines. Adamson's right hand went for his underarm holster, but his partner had gotten Murch in a bearhug and pulled. The front of the captive agent's coat tore away in his hands.

Adamson's chest heaved. He gestured with his revolver. "Get him the hell out of here." His voice cracked.

Murch struggled, but his right arm was yanked behind him and twisted. Pain shot through his shoulder. He went along, whimpering. Shoved out into the corridor, he had to run to catch his balance and slammed into the opposite wall, knocking a memo off a bulletin board. The door exploded shut.

A group of well-dressed men standing nearby stopped talking to look at him. He realized that he was still holding pieces of Adamson's jacket. He let them fall, brushed back his thinning hair with a shaky hand, adjusted his suit, and moved off down the corridor.

Redman and his lawyer were being interviewed on the courthouse steps by a TV crew. Murch gave them a wide berth on his way down. He overheard Redman telling the reporters he was leaving tomorrow for a week's vacation in Jamaica. Ice formed in the bookkeeper's stomach. Redman was giving himself an alibi for when Murch's body turned up.

Anyway, he had eighteen hours' grace. He decided to write off the stuff he had left back at the hotel and took a cab to his house on the west side. For years he had kept two thousand dollars in cash there in case he needed a getaway stake in a hurry. By the time he had his key in the front door lock he was already breathing easier; Redman's men wouldn't try anything until their boss was out of the country, and a couple of grand could get a man a long way in eighteen hours.

His house had been ransacked.

They had overlooked nothing. They had torn up the rugs, pulled apart the sofa and easy chairs and slit open the cushions, taken pictures down from the walls and dismantled the frames, removed the back panel from the TV set, dumped out the flour and sugar canisters in the kitchen. Even the plates had been unscrewed from the wall switches. The orange juice can in which he had kept the rolled bills in the freezer compartment of the refrigerator lay empty on the linoleum.

The sheer, cold logic of the operation dizzied Murch. Even after they had found the money they had gone on to make sure there were no other caches. His office alone, its contents smeared out into the passage that led to the stairs, would have taken hours to reduce to its present condition. The search had to have started well before the verdict was in, perhaps even as early as the weekend he had spent in that motel by the railroad tracks. Redman had been so confident of victory he had moved to cut off the bookkeeper's escape while the trial was still in progress.

He couldn't stay there. Probably he was already being watched, and the longer he remained the greater his chances of being kept prisoner in his own home until the word came down to eliminate him. He stepped outside. The street was quiet except for some noisy kids playing basketball in a neighbor's driveway and the snort of a power mower farther down the block. He started walking toward the corner.

Toward the bank. They'd taken his passbook, too, but he had better than six thousand in his account and he could borrow against that. Buy a used car or hop a plane. Maybe even go to Jamaica, stretch out on the beach next to Redman, and wait for his reaction. He smiled at that. Confidence warmed him, like whiskey in a cold belly. He mounted the bank steps, grasped the handle on the glass door. And froze.

He was alerted by the one reading a bank pamphlet in a chair near the door. There were no lines at the tellers' cages and no reason to wait. He spotted the other standing at the writing table, pretending to be making out a deposit slip. Their eyes wandered the lobby from time to time, casually. Murch didn't recognize their faces, but he knew the type: early thirties, jackets tailored to avoid telltale bulges. He reversed directions, moving slowly to keep from drawing attention. His heart started up again when he cleared the plate glass.

It was quarter to five, too late to reach another branch before closing, and even if he did he knew what would be waiting for him. He knew they had no intention of accosting him unless he tried to borrow money. They were running him like hounds, keeping him within range while they waited for the go-ahead. He was on a short tether with Redman on the other end.

But a man who juggled figures the way Much did had more angles than the Pentagon. He hailed a cruising cab and gave the driver Bart Morgan's address on Whitaker.

Morgan's laundromat was twice as big as the room in back where the real business was conducted, with a narrow office between to prevent the ringing of the telephones from reaching the housewives washing their husbands' socks out front. Murch found the proprietor there counting change at the card table he used for a desk. Muscular but running to fat, Morgan had crewcut steel-gray hair and wore horn-rimmed glasses with a hearing aid built into one bow. His head grew straight out of his T-shirt.

"How they running, Bar?"

"They need fixing." He reached across the stacked coins to shake Murch's hand.

"I meant the horses, not the machines."

"So did I."

They laughed. When they were through, Murch said, "I need money, Bart."

"I figured that." The proprietor's gaze dropped to the table. "You caught me short, Charlie. I got bit hard at the Downs Saturday."

"I don't need much, just enough to get out of the city."

"I'm strapped. I wish to hell I wasn't but I am." He took a quarter from one stack and placed it atop another. "You know I'd do it if I could."

The bookkeeper seized his wrist. "You owe me, Bart. If I didn't lend you four big ones when the Dodgers took the Series, you'd be part of an off-ramp by now."

"I paid back every cent."

"It ain't the money, it's the doing what's needed."

Morgan avoided his eyes. Murch cast away his friend's wrist.

"Redman's goons been here, ain't they?"

Their gazes met for an instant, then Morgan's dropped again. "I got a wife and a kid that can't stay out of trouble." He spoke quietly. "What they gonna do I don't come home some night, or the next or the next?"

"You and me are friends."

"You got no right to say that." Morgan's face grew red. "You got no right to come in here and ask me to put my chin on the block."

Murch slammed his fist on the table. Coins scattered. "If you don't give it to me I'll take it."

"I don't think so." Morgan leaned back, exposing a curved black rubber grip pressing into his paunch above the waistband of his pants.

Murch said, "You'd do Redman's job for him?"

"I'll do what I got to to live, same as you."

Telephones jangled in back, all but drowned out by the whooshing of the machines out front. The bookkeeper straightened. "Tell your wife and kid Charlie said good-bye." He went out, leaving the door open behind him.

"You got no right, Charlie."

Murch kept going. Morgan stood up, shouting over the racket of the front-loaders. "You should of come to me before you went running to the feds! I'd of give you the odds!"

His visitor was on the street.

Dusk was gathering when he left the home of his fourth and last friend in the city. His afflicted shoulder, inflamed by the humid weather and the rough treatment he'd received in Adamson's office, throbbed like an aching tooth. His hands were empty. Like Bart Morgan, Gordy Sharp and Ed Zimmer pleaded temporary poverty, Zimmer stepping out onto the porch to talk while his family remained inside. There was no answer at Henry Arbogast's, yet Murch swore he'd seen a light go off in one of the windows on his way up the walk.

Which left Liz.

He counted the money in his wallet. Forty-two dollars. He had spent almost thirty on cabs, leaving himself with just enough for a room for the night if he failed to get shut of the city. Liz was living in the old place two miles uptown. He sighed, put away the billfold, and planted the first sore foot on concrete.

Night crept out of the shadowed alleys to crouch beyond the pale rings cast by the street lights. He avoided them, taking his comfort in the invisibility darkness lent him. Twice he halted, breathing shallowly, when cars crawled along the curb going in his direction, then he resumed walking as they turned down side streets and picked up speed. His imagination flourished in the absence of light.

The soles of his feet were sending sharp pains splintering up through his ankles by the time he reached the brickfront apartment house and mounted the well-worn stairs to the fourth floor. Outside 4C he leaned against the wall while his breathing slowed and his face cooled. Straightening, he raised his fist, paused, and knocked gently.

A steel chain prevented the door from opening beyond the width of her face. Her features were dark against the light behind her, sharper than before, the skin creased under her eyes and at the corners of her mouth. Her black hair was streaked with dirty gray and needed combing. She'd aged considerably.

"I knew you'd show up," she snapped, cutting his greeting in half. "I heard about the verdict on the news. You want money."

"I'm lonesome, Liz. I just want to talk." He'd forgotten how quick she was. But he had always been able to soften her up in the past. Well, all but once.

"You never talked all time we was married unless you wanted something. I can't help you, Charlie." She started to close the door.

He leaned on it. His bad shoulder howled. "Liz, you're my last stop. They got all the other holes plugged." He told her about Adamson's broken promise, about the bank and his friends. "Redman'll kill me just to make an example."

She said, "And you're surprised?"

"What's that supposed to mean?" He controlled his anger with an effort. That had always been her chief weapon, her instinct for the raw nerve.

"There's two kinds in this world, the ones that use and the ones that get used." Her face was completely in shadow now, unreadable. "Guys like Redman and Adamson squeeze all the good out of guys like you and then throw you away. That's the real reason I divorced you, Charlie. You was headed for the junkpile the day you was born. I just didn't want to be there to see it."

"Christ, Liz, I'm talking about my life!"

"Me, too. Just a second." She withdrew, leaving the door open.

He felt the old warmth returning. Same old Liz: deliver a lecture, then turn around and come through after all. It was like enduring a sermon at the Perpetual Mission in return for a hot meal and a roof for the night.

"Here." Returning, she thrust a fistful of something through the opening. He reached for it eagerly. His fingers closed on cold steel.

"You nuts? I ain't fired a gun since the army!"

"It's all I got to give you. Don't let them find out where it came from."

"What good is it against a dozen men with guns?"

"No good, the way you're thinking. I wait tables in Redman's neighborhood. I hear things. He likes blowtorches. Don't let them burn you alive, Charlie."

She shut the door. The lock snapped with a noise like jaws closing.

It was a clear night. The Budweiser sign in the window of the corner bar might have been cut with an engraving tool out of orange neon. Someone gasped when he emerged from the apartment building. A woman in evening dress hurried past on a man's arm, her face tight and pale in the light coming out through the glass door, one brown eye rolling back at Murch. He'd forgotten about the gun. He put it away.

His subsequent pounding had failed to get Liz to open her door. If he'd wanted a weapon he'd have gotten it himself; the city bristled with unregistered iron. He fingered the unfamiliar thing in his pocket, wondering where to go next. His eyes came to the bright sign in the window.

Blood surged in his ears. Murch's robberies had all been from company treasuries, not people; his weapons figures in ledgers. Demanding money for lives required a steady hand and the will to carry out the threat. It was too raw for him, too much like crime. He started walking away from the bar. His footsteps slowed halfway down the block and stopped twenty feet short of the opposite corner. He turned around and retraced his steps. He was squeezing the concealed revolver so hard his knuckles ached.

The establishment was quiet for that time of the evening, deserted but for a young bartender in a red apron standing at the cash register. The jukebox was silent. As Murch approached, the employee turned unnaturally bright eyes on him. The light from the beer advertisement reflecting off the bar's cherrywood finish flushed the young man's face. "Sorry, friend, we're—"

Murch pointed the .38 at him. His hand shook.

The bartender smiled weakly.

"This ain't no joke! Get 'em up!" He tried to make his voice tough. It came out high and ragged.

Slowly the young man raised his hands. He was still smiling. "You're out of luck, friend."

Murch told him to shut up and open the cash register drawer. He obeyed. It was empty.

"Someone beat you to it, friend. Two guys with shotguns came in an hour ago, shook down the customers, and cleaned me out, even my wallet. Didn't even leave enough to open up with in the morning. You just missed the cops."

His smile burned. Murch's finger tightened on the trigger and the expression was gone. The bookkeeper backed away, bumped into a table. The gun almost went off. He turned and stumbled toward the door. He tugged at the handle; it didn't budge. The sign said PUSH. He shoved his way through to the street. Looking back, he saw the bartender dialing a telephone.

The night air stung Murch's face, and he realized there were tears on his cheeks. His thoughts fluttered wildly. He caught them and sorted them into piles with the discipline of one trained to work with assets and debits. Redman couldn't have known he would pick this particular bar to rob, even had he suspected the bookkeeper's desperation would make him choose that course. Blind luck had decided whom to favor, and as usual it wasn't Charlie Murch.

A distant siren awakened him to practicalities. Soon he would be a fugitive from the law as well as from Redman.

He pocketed the gun and ran.

His breath was sawing in his throat two blocks later when he spotted a cab stopped at a light. He sprinted across to it, tore open the back door, and threw himself into a seat riddled with cigarette burns.

"Off duty, bub," said the driver, hanging a puffy, stubbled face over the back of his seat. "Oil light's on. I'm on my way back to the garage."

There was no protective panel between the seats. He thrust the handgun in the driver's face and thumbed back the hammer.

The man sighed heavily. "All I got's twelve bucks and change. I ain't picked up a fare yet."

He was probably lying, but the light was green and Murch didn't want to be arrested arguing with a cabbie. "Just drive."

They passed a prowl car on its way toward the bar, its siren gulping, its lights flashing. Murch fought the urge to duck, hiding the gun instead. The county lock-up was full of men who would ice him just to get in good with Redman.

He got an idea that frightened him. He tried tucking it away, but it kept coming back.

"Mister, my engine's overheating."

Murch glanced up. The cab was making clunking noises. The warning light on the dash glowed angry red. They had gone nine blocks.

"All right, pull over."

The driver spun the wheel. As he rolled to a stop next to the curb the motor coughed, shuddered, and died. Steam rolled out from under the hood.

"Start counting." His passenger reached across the front seat and tore the microphone free of the two-way radio. "Don't get out till you reach a thousand. If you do, you won't have time to be sorry you did." He slid out and slammed the door on six.

He caught another cab four blocks over, this time without having to use force. It was a twenty-dollar ride out to the posh residential district where Jules Redman lived. He tipped the cabbie five dollars. He had no more use for money.

The house was a brick ranchstyle in a quiet cul-de-sac studded with shade trees. Murch found the hike to the front door effortless; for the first time in hours he was without pain. On the step he took a deep breath, let half of it out, and rang the bell. He took out the gun. Waited.

After a lifetime the door was opened by a very tall young man in a tan jacket custom made to contain his enormous chest. It was Randolph, Redman's favorite bodyguard. His eyes flickered when he recognized the visitor. A hand darted inside his jacket.

The reports were very loud. Murch fired a split second ahead of Randolph, shattering his sternum and throwing off his aim so that the second bullet entered the bookkeeper's left thigh. He'd never been shot before; it was oddly sensationless, like the first time he'd had sex. The bodyguard crumpled.

Murch stepped across him. He could feel the hot blood on his leg, nothing else. Just then Redman appeared in an open doorway beyond the staircase. When he saw Murch he froze. He was wearing a maroon velvet robe over pajamas and his feet were in slippers.

The bookkeeper was motionless as well. What now? He hadn't expected to get this far. He had shot Randolph in self-defense; he couldn't kill a man in cold blood, not even this one, not even when that was the fate he had planned for Murch.

Redman understood. He smiled under his moustache. "Like I said before, Charlie, you just don't live right."

Another large man came steadily through a side door, towed by the automatic pistol in his hand. He was older than Randolph and wore neither jacket nor necktie, his empty underarm holster exposed. This was the other bodyguard. He held up before the sight that met his eyes.

"Kill him, Ted."

Murch's bullet splintered one of the steps in the staircase. He'd aimed at the banister, but that was close enough. "Next one goes between your boss's eyes," he said.

Ted laid his gun on the floor and backed away from it, raising his hands.

The bookkeeper felt no triumph. He wondered if it was fear that was making him numb or if he just didn't care. To Redman: "Over there." He gestured with the .38 toward Randolph's gun where he'd dropped it when he fell.

The racketeer stayed put. "You're losing blood, Charlie."

"Shut up." He cocked the hammer.

Redman took a step toward the pistol.

"Pick it up. Slow," he added, as Redman stooped to obey.

He accepted the firearm with his free hand and dropped it carefully in a pocket to avoid smearing the fingerprints. To Ted: "Get the car."

Murch was waiting in front with his hostage when the bodyguard drove the Cadillac out of the garage. "Okay, get out."

Ted slid out from under the wheel. Murch made Redman take his place and climbed in on the passenger's side. "Start driving. I'll tell you what turns to make." He spoke through clenched teeth. His leg was starting to ache and he was feeling lightheaded.

In the side mirror, the bodyguard stood watching them until they reached the end of the driveway. Then he swung around and sprinted back inside.

"He'll be on the phone to the others in two seconds," Redman said. "How far you think you'll get before you bleed out?"

"Turn right."

The big car took the bumps well. Even so, each one was like a red-hot knife in his thigh. He made himself as comfortable as possible without taking his eyes off the driver, the revolver resting in his lap with his hand on the butt. He welcomed Redman's taunts. They distracted him from his pain, kept his mind off the drowsiness welling up inside him like warm water filling a tub. He wasn't so far from content.

The dead bodyguard would take explaining. But a paraffin test would reveal that he'd fired a weapon recently, and the gun in Murch's pocket was likely registered to Randolph. Redman's prints on the butt and the fact the dead man had worked for him, together with the bullet in Murch's leg and a clear motive in his testimony in the bribery trial, would put his old boss inside for a long time for attempted murder. "Left here."

The lights of the Fourteenth Precinct were visible down the block. Detective Sergeant Kirdy's precinct, the home of the kind, proud grandfather who had protected Murch during the trial. Murch told Redman to stop the car. It felt good to give him that last order.

Charlie Murch had stopped being one of the used.

He recognized Kirdy's blocky shape hastily descending the front steps as he followed Redman out the driver's side and called to him. The sergeant shielded his eyes with one hand against the glare of the headlights, squinted at the two figures coming toward him, one limping, the other in a bathrobe being pushed out ahead. He drew his Magnum from his belt holster. Murch gestured to show friendship. The noise the policeman's gun made was deafening, but Murch never heard it.

"That was quick thinking, Sergeant." Hands in the pockets of his robe, Redman looked down at Murch's body spread-eagled in the gutter. A crowd was gathering.

"We got the squeal on your kidnapping a few minutes ago," Kirdy said. "I was just heading out there when you two showed."

"You ought to make lieutenant for this."

The sergeant's kind eyes glistened. "That'd be great, Mr. Redman. The wife and kids been after me for years to get off the street."

"You will if there's any justice. How's that pretty granddaughter of yours, by the way?"

# Bad Blood

*This one is an exercise in style; the ironic twist came as a surprise even to me.*

Light spread gray through the sycamores, igniting billions of hanging droplets with the black trunks standing among them looking not fixed to the earth but suspended from above like stalactites. A mockingbird awoke to release its complex scan into the sopping air. There was no answer and the song was not repeated. Leaves crackled, drying.

The man was already awake, a tense silhouette against a yellowing sun louvered by vertical tree shafts, a knee on the ground, the other drawn up to his chest and one fist wrapped around a rifle with its butt planted in the moist earth. His profile was sharp, with a pointed nose like a check mark, the angle dramatized by a long stiff bill tilting down from a green cap with JOHN DEERE embossed in block letters in a patch on the front of the crown. His shirt was coarse and blue under a red-and-black-checked jacket with darns on the elbows. His jeans had been blue but were now earth-colored, like his boots under their cake of silver clay. He had been there in that position since an hour before dawn.

From where he was crouched, the ground fell off forty-five degrees to a berry thicket that girdled the mountain. The thicket had been transplanted by his great-grandfather from a nearby bog and allowed to grow wild until it resembled the tangled barbed wire in which the great-grandfather's son would snare himself thirty years later and wait for the Germans to discover him in a muddy place called Ypres. This natural barrier had trapped a number of local men the same way, to wait like the soldier and, now, like the soldier's grandson for the dawn and what the dawn would bring. The slope bristled with leafed trees and cedars and twisted jack pines, heirs to the great towering monarchs that had fallen to the timber boom of another century. Their black stumps still dotted the mountainside like rotted teeth.

A third of the way down the slope, a hundred feet below him and two hundred feet above the thicket, stood his own shack. It had been built of logs when James Monroe was president, but a later ancestor had nailed clapboard over the logs to make it resemble a proper house. A four-paned window that had been covered with oiled paper before the coming of the railroad now reflected sunlight from three panes, emphasizing the blank space where a bullet had shattered the glass.

Now, as the sun lifted, its light struck sparks off tiny fragments on his jeans. He flicked them away carefully. Before tumbling out of the shack he had made sure to remove his wristwatch and anything else that might catch light and betray him.

He knew who had fired the bullet. Inside the shack, its cracked black cover freshly nicked by that same projectile, lay a Bible as thick as a man's thigh, its cream flyleaves scribbled over in old brown ink with names of his forebears and the dates of their births and deaths going back to 1789, when an indentured servant from Cornwall bought the book secondhand in London and recorded the birth of a son named Jotham. Four generations of names followed before the simple entry: "Eben Candler, murdered by Ezekiel Finlayson, Hawkins County, Kentucky, May 11, 1882. His will be done." Eighteen similar notations appeared on succeeding pages, in differing hands, until the survivors wearied of keeping count. The final line, "Jotham Edward Candler, born September 8, 1951," written in his father's formal script, commemorated his own birth. Finlayson losses were not included.

No one remembered the specifics of that first encounter between a Candler and a Finlayson, although it had something to do with the ownership of forty acres of bottomland in Unicoi County. Only the casualties were remembered. Jotham's own coming of age had been marked by a daily catechism in which he was expected to recite, in whatever order asked, the names of the Candler slain, their murderers, and the dates of their deaths as they had been recorded in the big Bible; and when he was strong enough to lift a squirrel rifle, he had been taught to think of his small, furry targets not as squirrels but as Finlaysons.

It did not matter that no one knew who held title to those forty acres—that was as gone as the bottomland itself, seized by the bank during the Panic of 1893—or that the fecundity of the Candler and Finlayson women had led to considerable interbreeding between the two families during the long truces. Hatred was an inheritance as solid and treasured as the old Bible and Great-Grandmother Candler's homely samplers, their red embroidery and white linen gone the same dead-skin brown on the walls of the tiny shack. Jotham, with a bachelor's degree in agriculture and three years in Vietnam behind him, was growing marijuana on plots that had supported his father's stills, and the Finlaysons had sold Ezekiel's farrier's shop to buy a funeral home and the first of a chain of hardware stores, but aside from that little had changed. Bad blood was bad always.

As the sun cleared the mountain, its light turned leafy green coming down through the branches. Creatures stirred in the dry-shuck mattress of last year's leaves, and the last wisp of woodsmoke left the shack's chimney in a bit of shredded tissue that vanished into the thatch of fog now treetop-high as it lifted and broke apart. Jotham's assailant would know by that that he was no longer inside. The waiting had almost ended.

Jotham was the last Candler to bear that surname. His sisters were married and his only brother had died in Korea before Jotham was old enough to remember him. He would carry the name to the grave with him because of what the army's defoliants had done to his genes in Da Nang. In view of that temptation—the opportunity to wipe out by one death the long line of Candlers—young Bertram Finlayson's attempt to kill him in his sleep that morning seemed long overdue.

He had no doubt it was Bertram. Eight years Jotham's junior, he had been too young to serve in Vietnam, and had spent that frustration in turkey shoots across the state, winning a caseful of trophies to display under the antlered heads on the walls of his fine house in town. His arsenal was a legend among collectors of firearms and he often boasted that he had used them to kill every kind of animal that lived in the county but one. He was the only Finlayson young enough and mean enough to bother about a fight that most had thought was buried with Jotham's father.

Several times since Jotham had returned from college on the G.I. Bill, Bertram had tried to draw him into something in town, from which Jotham had always walked away. Witnesses said it was because he had had enough of killing in Asia. But those who said that were thinking of other wars, did not understand that the object of his had been to stay alive; killing came secondary, if at all. And now here he was, twelve years and ten thousand miles later, trying to stay alive in another jungle.

A squirrel began chattering, a high-pitched coughing noise like a small engine trying to start. Something was annoying it. Not him; the squirrel was too far away, high in an ash on the other side of the shack. He spotted its humped profile on the side of the trunk sixty feet up and scanned the ground at the base. A treefall twenty yards down the slope looked promising. He raised the .30-06, lined up the iron sights, and sent a bullet into the center of the fall. Something jumped, startled. Dead leaves rattled on the inert branches.

The echo of his first report was still snarling in the distance when he fired again, into those moving leaves. Almost instantly, a section of bark on a cedar a foot to Jotham's right exploded in a cloud of splinters, followed quickly by the crack of a .30-30. He hurled himself and his weapon headlong down the slope, rolling and coming up on the other side of a clump of suckers grown up around a pine stump. The squirrel had stopped chattering.

Bertram was a cooler hand than he'd thought. After the first shot he had waited, then fired at Jotham's second muzzle flash.

Again the waiting began.

Once, after exchanging fire with a Cong he had never seen, Jotham had waited for eleven hours in a fog of mosquitoes and heavy air, unmoving, his survival dependent upon his either killing the guerrilla or boring him into moving on. At the end the Cong had lost patience first, and when he rose from cover to investigate, Jotham had taken his head off with a burst from his M-16. How to wait was the hardest lesson of all. He settled himself on the other knee to give that haunch a rest.

The sun climbed into a thin sheeting of clouds that parted from time to time, changing the light as in an ancient motion picture. The air warmed, grew hot and thick. Twice he was attacked by wood ticks, once on the back of a hand, the other time, very painfully, on his neck. He did not move to brush them away. Eventually they'd crawled off drunkenly, bloated with his blood.

When the sun was directly overhead, he knew a terrible urge to get up and find out if Bertram was still there. More than the heat, it made the sweat stand out in burrs on his forehead and greased his armpits and crotch. It must have been what the Cong had felt just before he committed suicide. But Jotham held his position and it subsided.

No one came up the mountain. In other years, uninvited visitors had met moonshiners' buckshot, and now even the authorities counseled against wandering the hills and chancing the protective wrath of marijuana growers and mad survivalists.

Around midafternoon the sky darkened and big drops pattered the leaves on the ground and rolled along the edge of the bill of Jotham's cap and hung quivering before falling to his raised thigh with loud plops. He swung the rifle horizontal to keep moisture out of the barrel. But the rain passed swiftly. A rainbow arched over the shack and melted away.

The air cooled toward dusk. Bertram would have to move soon. Jotham's new knowledge of his enemy's instincts told him that he would not again risk darkness in the woods with an experienced jungle fighter. Jotham reversed legs again, working the stiffness out of the long muscles in his thighs.

The woods to the west were catching fire in the lowering sun when a buck mule deer that Jotham had never heard went crashing off through the trees on the opposite side of the shack, blatting a warning to others of its kind. At that moment the treefall shook and a pair of bull shoulders with a hatless head nestled in between reared against a sky striped with tree trunks. Light sheared along something long and shiny.

Jotham raised his rifle without aiming, trusting to the barrel to find its mark because he could no longer see the front sight, and touched the trigger. The butt pulsed against his shoulder, but he did not hear the blast. It had been that way when he'd killed the Cong. In roaring silence the bull shoulders hunched and the hatless head went back and the silhouette crumpled in on itself like a balloon deflating. The long and shiny thing flashed, falling.

Jotham let the sun slip to a red crescent before rising. In gray light he approached the treefall, lifting his feet clear of the old stumps more from memory than from sight, his eyes fixed on the dark thing draped over the fallen tree with the .30-30 on the ground in front of it. Carefully he used a foot to slide the rifle farther out of the reach of the dangling hands, then took another step and grasped a handful of straw-colored hair and raised a slack face with open eyes and mouth into the last ray of light. It was Bertram Finlayson.

He let the face drop and started down the mountain toward town to tell his sister Lucy that she was a widow.

# Cabana

*When the old* The Armchair Detective *decided to publish fiction, I was offered a tempting fee to take part. I was jammed up and begged for time. That night, I dreamed the following story, something that had never happened before. I awoke with the plot all laid out, and wrote it in three hours. But the really inexplicable thing is I'd had no previous exposure to anything remotely resembling it when I went to bed.*

*Amusing aside: Petitioned by* AD *for permission to illustrate the story with a photo from its archives, the Brazilian tourism commission asked to see the story, to ensure it didn't paint a bleak picture of Rio. Its request was granted—and its permission to use the photo withheld.*

Hale thanked me for the glass of water and used it to chase down a yellow pill the size of a cuff link.

"I'm on medication," he told me helpfully. "I will be for the rest of my life, I guess. That's a tough admission to make at my age."

I figured that to be around twenty-five. He was a small, slender specimen with fragile wrists and features and thick black hair cut short up front and long in the back, the way they're wearing it now. He looked healthy enough. He had the sinews of a runner under his tennis shirt and shorts.

"What've you got?" I refilled my glass from the pitcher of martinis on the wicker table, no pill.

"It has a Latin name I can't pronounce. As I understand it, it's a benign growth on my brain, hanging down like a stalactite at the base of the occipital lobe. Without the medication, any exertion or great shock can cause it to move and touch my spinal column. I black out. Afterward I can't remember anything from a few minutes before the blackout. I'm told I become abusive, even violent."

"And *with* the medication?"

"I'm a little better. Do you know where Sharon is, Mr. Gardener?"

I looked past him at the ocean. Nothing new there. At that hour of the afternoon it was teal-blue, the long swells coming in like wind blowing across satin and creaming on the beach. I'd been living in the little cabana behind me for two years and nothing ever changed, not the ocean or the throbbing blue sky or the growling and honking of Rio beyond the palms on the hill.

"I found her," I said, "I think. I've sent someone to confirm her address. Come back tomorrow morning and I'll have it for you."

He gulped down the rest of his water. "I was told you work alone."

"I farm out some of the grunt work. Don't worry. He doesn't know about Detroit."

"I shouldn't have told *you*. I still don't know how you got it out of me."

"Relax. There's no extradition between the United States and Brazil. At least half the people I work for are thieves. Most of them are like you, amateurs who embezzled a bundle in one shot and took off with the briefcase for romantic Rio. Amateur thieves fall into patterns. I needed to know she was one before I started looking."

"Sharon isn't a thief," he said. "Not really. I took that money. She didn't even know about it until we were in the air, on our way to a two-week vacation in South America; or so she thought."

"Plenty of women here. Why bring her at all?"

"We were going to be married. We still are, if I can find her and apologize. I—had an episode. In the Rio de Janeiro airport. I woke up in jail. The officers told me I tried to tear the place apart. Sharon was gone. So was the suitcase and six hundred thousand dollars."

"And you want to apologize to *her*?"

"I must have frightened her. She never saw one of my spells before. I was nervous; I forgot to take my medication. That was two weeks ago. She must be terrified, with all that money in a strange country and no way to get back home. She'd be afraid to buy a ticket with stolen bills."

My glass was empty again; evaporation's a problem in Brazil. I filled it again and drank. I felt the familiar gnawing at my ulcer. "Is it her you want, or the money?"

"Both. I love Sharon, but I threw away my career for the money. What good's a career if this tumor turns malignant? If I'm going to die young, I want to be in a villa overlooking the ocean with the woman I love at my side."

"Romantic. Come back tomorrow morning."

The sun was barely over the sill when someone banged on the cabana door. I stumbled to the window in my shorts and looked out at Hale standing on the little flagged patio where we'd sat the previous afternoon. The pitcher with its puddle of melted ice looked sad.

"Have you got it?" he demanded when I opened the door. Today he had on a Sea Island shirt over white flannels.

I gave him the address. "It belongs to a cabana like this one. It's a twenty-minute drive down the coast. Want me to go with you?"

"No, thanks." He handed me an envelope full of cash. He watched me count it. "Are you all right, Gardener?"

"Damn ulcers kept me up all night."

"You ought to give up drinking."

"What else is there to do down here?"

He thanked me for my good work and left. The wheels of his rented Jeep spun and spat sand.

I gave him five minutes, then dressed and went after him in my Mexican Oldsmobile.

The cabana was about the same size as mine, but nicer, with a red Spanish tile roof and recent white paint on the stucco. There was a little flower garden in front, professionally tended. Nice view of the ocean out back. Apparently Sharon didn't mind spending stolen money on overhead as much as she did using it to buy a ticket home; but that had been Hale's assessment, and he was no judge of character. His Jeep was parked in front.

The front door stood wide open. Inside, the place looked like hurricane footage: furniture dumped over, cushions slashed and bleeding white cotton batting, holes kicked in the plaster. Hale was sitting on the floor in the middle of it all, next to the woman's body. She had on a halter top, shorts, and sandals. She had been a pretty blonde before someone had caved in her face with something hard and heavy.

He looked up at me. I could see his skull through his pale skin. "Did I—? Did I—?"

"Black out? I guess so." I leaned down, felt the woman's throat, and wiped my hand on my pants. "She's dead, okay. You want to tell me anything?"

"I don't remember. I don't—I wouldn't hurt Sharon."

I said nothing. He saw where I was looking and glanced down at the object in his hand. It was a stone carving of one of the Inca gods like you find in the better souvenir shops, plastered with blood. He dropped it as if it had suddenly sprung to life.

"That'd do it," I said, nodding. "You'd better get up. We'll figure out something to tell the cops. They're down on *norteamericanos* here, importing their troubles to peaceful Brazil." I held out my hand.

He stared at it for a moment, as a dog will. Then he grasped it. He was almost upright when I stuck the little Czech automatic into his belly and pulled the trigger three times.

The cabana had no telephone, so I walked down the beach and gave a dollar to one of the boys who sell Pizarro's sunken gold to fetch an officer. Then I went back inside to wait.

I hadn't counted on the shock of his finding Sharon's body triggering one of Hale's blackouts, but it didn't matter. Even if he never remembered being innocent of her murder, he wouldn't forget the money. I'd spent most of the night looking for it after I'd killed her, and had only just gotten back to my cabana with it and undressed for bed when he banged on the door. It was a good set-up, considering how little time I'd had to rig it after I found out about Hale's condition. The medical examiners in Rio are among the best in the world; once a thorough autopsy brought his tumor to light, I'd have no trouble convincing the authorities I'd shot him in self-defense when he attacked me after bludgeoning the girl to death in one of his blind rages.

By the time they found out about the six hundred thousand, I'd be out of this country, with its unchanging sky and monotonous surf and too many thieves.

# Lock, Stock, and Casket

*When the commercial publications begged off, I placed this one with a dusty literary magazine, which is a sign of shabby honor in certain circles. I think what makes this kind of story work is the wisdom behind proving motivation in court: In order for the jury to convict the defendant, it must on some level understand the reason behind the crime, and agree with it.*

People who didn't know that Umberto Fugurello was a great artist tended to mistake him for a comical old man. Outside his shop, his was a rheumatic figure smaller than the average in a tight black coat buttoned at the neck and a gray Homburg perched atop wild gray hair like an egg in a nest. Below that were gold-rimmed spectacles, a tight, lipless mouth, and a chin that usually wore a Band-Aid to remind him that one can get only so many shaves out of a razor before it becomes a lethal weapon.

In the shop, he was a professional in leather apron and shirt-sleeves, the cuffs rolled up past corded forearms ending in large hands cracked and discolored by the many stains and acids with which he worked. The walls and benches twinkled with mallets, chisels, miters, and wood augers of spotless nickel steel, no two of which were designed for the same purpose. Their handles were worn to fit the contours of Umberto's calloused fingers and no one else's.

Umberto Fugurello made caskets. So had every previous male Fugurello back to Great-Great-Grandfather Filberto Gugliano, who, legend said, crafted the final resting place of Catherine de Medici. Since then, many another famous figure had gone to his reward in vessels fashioned by the Stradivari of caskets, and Umberto, had he been a boastful man, could point with pride to mausolea and family vaults throughout both hemispheres in which resided the evidence of his clan's skill.

But it was generally agreed within the closed ranks of the world's casket makers that Umberto was the best of his line. Who could forget the Egyptian-style sarcophagus he had designed for the eminent archaeologist Professor Simon Broderick, dead of a hitherto unknown Middle Eastern strain of venereal disease, or the gold inlays around the lid of the box in which Dirk Crandall, the motion picture star, was buried after his wife caught him rehearsing a love scene from his latest movie with a studio switchboard operator, or the lion motif Umberto had created for famed animal trainer Hugo von Rasmussen, following that tragic episode involving a young Siberian tiger the performer had mistaken for an aging Bengal? There was in addition the double-decked piece he had built on commission for a local Syndicate chief, but that was known only to Umberto himself, and he was not one to brag.

In any case, past triumphs meant nothing to him. He lived in the present. And why not, in view of the fact that he was working on his masterpiece?

It lay across two sawhorses in the back room of the shop, a lozenge-shaped construction of forbidden hardwood from the Brazilian rainforest without a nail or a corner or a sharp edge anywhere. The handles were solid gold, the lining deep blue satin. The crowning touch—the Fugurello family crest, a hammer in a mailed fist framed in a coffin—was assuming definition even now at the point of Umberto's chisel. It surpassed all his earlier achievements, and certainly nothing would ever rival it in the future.

For this was to be his own casket.

The imminence of death hardly saddened him. He was seventy-eight, after all, and more aware than most that no one lived forever. His only regret was that he would be unable to observe the reaction to his last and greatest work when it was unveiled at his funeral. He was lamenting this necessary disappointment when the little bell mounted on the front door of the shop announced a visitor.

"Uncle Umberto?"

*Bastardo.*

The old man drew a tarpaulin over the casket just as his nephew, the mortician, entered through the curtain that separated the two rooms. The visitor was tall and thin—one was tempted to say "cadaverous"—and wore his dark hair fashionably long. Recent cosmetic surgery on his nose had left him with average features dominated by ice blue eyes that matched his suit.

"Good morning, Antonio."

"Tony." Something like annoyance edged the young man's cool tone. "Tony Farrell. I had it changed, remember?"

"Who could forget?" The decision to forsake the honored family name had undoubtedly contributed to the early demise of Antonio's father, brother of Umberto. "What brings you to my shop on a Saturday morning?"

"You mean *my* shop."

His uncle said nothing. That had been a great mistake, his deeding the property over to his brother's son on the occasion of his birth. Umberto had not touched wine since that night.

Antonio said, "A fellow has a right to inspect his possession from time to time. What's this, another masterpiece?" Before Umberto could stop him he reached over and pulled off the tarpaulin.

For a moment the beauty of the thing struck even his nephew. But he recovered himself quickly.

"What good will that do anyone when he's in the ground? What did I tell you about throwing money away on materials we don't need?"

"My money, not yours. The materials come out of my savings."

"And whose time did you spend on it? I heard you were turning down business, but I didn't believe it until now. That's the family crest on the lid. What were you going to do, enter it in some fool exhibition put on by those graveworms you call your colleagues?"

Umberto made no reply. In a twinkling, Antonio's manner went from hot to cold. "We'll talk about this later. I came down here to tell you I'm selling the shop."

"Selling!" The old man pronounced it as if it were an unfamiliar word.

"Lock, stock, and casket. I'm liquidating the inventory and putting the building and property on the open market. That includes your little project here. It should bring several thousand once we scrape off the engraving."

"The Fugurellos have been in this business for—"

"Too long. It's called moving with the times. No one does business with independents any more. They go to the big supply houses, where they can get machine-made models for a fraction of what you charge. This is a prime location for a parking garage. Of course, that means tearing down the building, but that shouldn't cost too much. A swift kick will do it. I'll make a killing."

"And me, Antonio?"

"Tony."

"Will you tear me down too, or sell me along with the inventory?"

His nephew smiled—a mortician's smile, blandly obsequious.

"Certainly not, Uncle. You've worked hard all your life; you've earned a rest. I've made arrangements with the Waning Years Retirement Home. You move in next week."

"But I don't want to retire!"

"What you want or don't want is not an issue. As your only living relative, I can have you declared incapable of caring for yourself and commit you to a state institution. Instead, I've elected to place you in private hands. You should be grateful."

"I'll fight you! I'll hire a lawyer."

"And what will you use to pay him? You don't even own these tools—which, by the way, I have a buyer for, if you can provide a list of what you have here. If you can't, I'll just make one." He produced a pad and pencil.

"I have rights."

"Not if you're senile, and that's what I'll prove in court if you insist upon making things difficult. This is a young man's world, Uncle. If you hadn't been so busy making your petty boxes you'd know that. Now, try to stay out of my way while I inventory this equipment." He started counting the braces and bits on the wall behind the lathe, tallying them into his pad.

Umberto glared at his nephew's back. Then his eyes fell to his masterpiece's unfinished crest, and as always when he contemplated a project, all other cares receded. He picked up the No. 5 hammer he'd been using, thought better of it, exchanged it for a heavier No. 3 with a shiny neoprene grip, and brought it down with all his might, squarely into the center of Antonio's fashionable hairstyle.

The Fugurello sanity hearing is in the records for anyone who cares to review it. Following conflicting testimonies by the psychiatrists who had examined the defendant, a harried judge ruled him legally insane and unfit for trial and committed him to the state mental institution for treatment. This failed to cheer Umberto, who was depressed by his inability to attend his nephew's celebrated funeral.

The centerpiece was the talk of his profession for weeks. Under a rose-colored spot, the casket's eggshell finish threw off a high gleam that put the flowers to shame. Everyone agreed that Antonio had never looked better, and when the service was over and the top half of the lid was lowered, exposing the ornate crest, the guests were moved in spite of the solemnity of the occasion to applaud.

After eighteen months, authorities at the institution agreed that Umberto could be trusted with tools once again, and he was granted permission to perform light work in the shop. These were happy days for Umberto, who had been cheered by his colleagues' letters and telegrams of congratulation upon his masterpiece; doing work he loved, he no longer thought about death or its proximity.

The doctors had, in fact, given him a clean bill of health, which he attributed to freedom from the responsibility of earning a living.

Then came the untimely passing of the institution's director and a special request for Umberto to craft a vessel for the remains. Material posed a problem in the face of bureaucratic cutbacks, but with effort he managed to obtain some good cedar and recycled brass for the handles and fittings. Making something worthwhile out of such second-class stock was a challenge he welcomed.

He rubbed the last irregularity from the surface and stood back to survey his workmanship. The trimming glittered like gold against the deep red-brown of the wood. He frowned appreciably at his reflection in the finish. It wasn't a masterpiece, but it was still good craftsmanship, and that was something money couldn't buy.

# Diminished Capacity

*I grew up among members of the Greatest Generation, and always felt closer to them than to my fellow boomers. There's just something about underestimated old age that brings out some of my best stories. . . .*

I was halfway through my third ham sandwich when the intercom on my desk razzed. Angrily, I choked down the mouthful I was working on and punched the speaker button, which was too small for my rather large thumb.

"Sharon, I thought I told you never to interrupt my lunch."

"Sorry, Matt." The mechanical voice coming from the speaker didn't sound sorry. The inference was that a man in my condition could afford to have his lunch interrupted now and then. "Seth Borden is here to see you. I thought you might be interested."

I sat back for a moment, frowning. A trip to Las Vegas for Dickens's venerable Miss Havisham was easier to envision than a visit from Seth Borden. He was the last person in Roseacre I would have expected to need an attorney.

"Herd him in." I rewrapped the uneaten portion of my sandwich and put it away in the file drawer, sweeping crumbs in after it off the desk top. By that time my visitor was standing awkwardly just inside the door.

Seth was older than the woodwork in the office and looked it. Little and wizened—"elfin," the Sunday supplement writers would call him—he wore gold-rimmed spectacles on a bent nose, a white shirt, and fuzzy gray pin-striped trousers under a leather apron streaked liberally with grease. His face and his white tousled hair and his hands were no cleaner, the hands calloused and stained a permanent brown from the many compounds and acids with which he worked. He looked out of place, as he would anywhere but amid the general disarray of his little workshop on Main Street.

I winched myself out of my chair and took his hand. It was warm and a little sticky. "Hello, Seth. Have a seat." I indicated the client's chair on his side of the desk.

He shook his head. "Can't stay. Got me some glue drying on two sticks of white pine and can't let it set no longer'n ten minutes. I come to hire you, if you're in the mood for it." He fished a scrap of paper out of an apron pocket and handed it to me.

It was a subpoena ordering him to appear in court in two weeks to show cause why he shouldn't be institutionalized under the law regarding diminished capacity, filed by his daughter. Her name was typed at the bottom of the sheet: Mrs. C. Burton Scott. I gave it back. "What brought this on?"

"It's her husband put her up to it," he said. "When I refused to sell my shop to that developing firm of his, he got himself a lawyer and between them they cooked up this thing that says I'm crazy and should be committed. June always did do what Burton told her, so he got her to sign this here complaint. Once I'm out of the way, the shop's hers, and they can do what they want with it."

He seemed more sad than angry, which was like him. People like Seth Borden live their lives never believing they'll get hurt. They get hurt a lot.

The scenario made sense. No one who lived in Roseacre could recall a time when Seth's shop wasn't there. Dwarfed though it was by skyscrapers, the little brick structure occupied a substantial part of the business district and was worth hundreds of thousands to the developer fortunate enough to acquire it. Knowing what I did about C. Burton Scott, I wondered why I hadn't seen this coming.

Not that no one had tried before. Twenty years earlier, Bedelia Borden, Seth's sister and partner by grace of their father's will, had tried to bully Seth into selling her his half so that she could make a bundle from a man who wanted to buy up the block and build a department store. Her constant browbeating had made her brother miserable and may have led to his wife Ruth's fatal heart attack at age forty-two. Bedelia might have won, having thus broken her brother's spirit, had not a severe recurrence of her childhood asthma forced her to abandon her interest and move to a dryer climate. No one had heard from her since and it was believed that she had died out West. Now the property was worth ten times what had been offered then.

The worst part was that in our state, the mere question of a person's sanity raised by his heirs was sufficient to go to court. Then it was a matter of which psychiatrist was more eloquent in expressing his opinions. Neither medicine nor the law is an exact science.

"Any reason to doubt your sanity, Seth?" I asked.

He shrugged; a gesture not calculated to win a lawyer's confidence.

"I forget things. Who don't? But I pay my bills and I run my business and I don't keep my socks in the icebox like my Uncle Ralph started doing just before he died. *You* think I'm crazy?" His eyes were sharp behind the spectacles.

"I'm not a psychiatrist. But I think I can help you. First I think we should discuss my fee."

Before I could continue, the old man reached into another pocket, brought out a fat handful of greasy, dog-eared bills, and dumped them on my desk. I counted them. They came to twenty-three hundred dollars in twenties and fifties.

"I was saving up for a new delivery van," he said. "I'll be in the shop when you want me." He left, presumably to see to his two sticks of wood.

Mr. and Mrs. C. Burton Scott lived north of the city along Route 22, in one of a string of neat little homes with neat little lawns and a big car in every driveway. I swung my Japanese puddle-jumper in behind a blue Seville and climbed out, sweating as soon as I left the air-conditioned interior. It was late August and fat men were out of season.

June Borden Scott answered the door on my second knock. She was a small woman of thirty, attractive enough, but there was too much of her Aunt Bedelia in her face to suit me. As a boy I had seen the old harridan once or twice and gone home feeling chilled. "Yes?" Her voice was thin, almost nonexistent.

I said, "I'm looking for Mr. Scott. Someone at his office said he was having lunch at home. I tried to call, but your number's unlisted. Matt Lysander. I think your husband remembers me."

He remembered me. Three seconds after June withdrew, he came storming up with fists clenched and stuck his big chin in my face. The rest of him was big, too, but I had eighty pounds on him, not that I cared to use them; he was all muscle. The shiny blue suits he always wore gave him an armored look. I'd noticed that in court, the day I persuaded a judge to fine Scott Developments fifty thousand dollars for using substandard materials in its construction. His appeal was still pending.

"What the hell do you want?"

"Relax; this visit won't cost you a cent." Twisting the knife is one of my specialties. "I'm representing Seth Borden. Let's talk."

His expression changed from belligerent to uncertain. At length he stepped aside to admit me.

The living room was sunken, professionally decorated and, I suspected, soundproof. I sat down in a brown crushed-leather chair without waiting for an invitation and stood my briefcase—an expensive prop—on the floor next to it. Scott took a seat beside his wife on the sofa opposite, but he didn't relax. He sat on the edge as if crouched to spring; that a man should do that in his own home I'd always found significant. *Mrs.* Scott looked like a frightened hamster in his presence. She'd inherited nothing of her Aunt Bedelia's overbearing manner.

I began without preamble. "Mrs. Scott, what makes you think your father is senile?"

Her husband started to answer for her. I held up a hand and he closed his mouth.

"He's—well, he has lapses," she began haltingly. "I invite him to dinner and he doesn't show up. When I called him to ask why, he says he never received an invitation."

"How many times has this happened?"

"I don't know. Three times, I guess. Perhaps four. All in the past couple of months."

"That hardly indicates failing faculties," I said. "I've forgotten my share of invitations, mainly because I was too polite to say I didn't feel like going."

"Oh, but that's not all! Just last week when I was shopping, Father walked right past me on the street without stopping to say hello. I had to call him twice before he recognized me. His own daughter!"

"Perhaps he was preoccupied."

Scott snorted. "What's he got to be preoccupied in his work?"

I ignored him.

"Let me ask you this, Mrs. Scott. Were you concerned about your father's mental condition before you related these incidents to your husband?"

*"Don't answer that!"*

Scott was standing, his beefy face red and turned upon me. "You can leave here on your own two feet or head first, Lysander. Your choice. I don't have to listen to this sort of thing in my own house."

"You will in court." I rose, facing him. "Let's be honest. All you've got is a couple of incidents of absent-mindedness a first-year law student could tear apart, and even then it's your word against Borden's. My psychiatrist will examine him, the state's psychiatrist will examine him, they'll each find exactly what they want to find, and they'll cancel each other out in court. In the end all you'll gain is a whopping bill from your lawyer, possibly court costs too, and no title to Seth's shop. Still want to go through with it?"

The obstinate expression remained on Scott's face, but his shoulders sank ever so slightly. "None of this would be necessary if the old fool would just sell." He was still angry, but not at me. "Did he tell you what I offered him for that pile of bricks?"

I said he hadn't. Scott quoted an amount. My surprise must have showed, because he inflated before my eyes.

"You see?" he roared. "I have a syndicate behind me, with money to burn. Would you turn down a chance to retire and never have to worry about money for the rest of your life? Borden did, and without blinking. If that isn't evidence of diminished capacity, you tell me what is!"

I picked up my briefcase, composing myself. A lawyer's first duty is to do what he can to keep his client out of court, and I'd given it my best shot. "Don't say I didn't warn you when the judge speaks his piece."

Mrs. Scott accompanied me to the door. Her face showed strain.

"It's true what Burton said," she whispered. "He wouldn't have gone out on a limb like that with his investors if it weren't my father. I know what you think of me. I'm sure it's what the whole town will be thinking when this gets out, but it isn't true. I just want to do what's best for Father, put him someplace where he won't harm himself. He won't move in here, he was adamant about that.

"I worry about him, all alone among those power tools. You can see that, can't you?"

I went out without committing myself.

Back at my office, I asked Sharon to get Fred Petrillo on the line. Fred was an assistant to an assistant at the State Bureau of Records and owed me a favor.

"Fred, this is Matt Lysander. Can you find out for me who C. Burton Scott's partners are over at Scott Developments?"

"I wasn't aware he had partners."

"Nor was I until about half an hour ago. A man who balks at a fifty-thousand-dollar fine doesn't make the kind of money offer he just told me about without wincing. Someone's backing his play."

"I'll get right on it. Hour soon enough?"

"Dandy." I hung up, wolfed down a candy bar for energy, and beat it down to Seth Borden's shop.

The proprietor was in back, refinishing an old desk that hardly seemed worth the bother. The floor around his feet was a litter of discarded tools under a mulch of wood shavings. A bare bulb swung from a cord above his head, slinging shadows over the cold walls. They weren't as ancient as they appeared. A couple of decades earlier, Seth had turned bricklayer and had redone the whole shop from top to bottom. But like everything else about him, his remodeling carried a built-in patina of age that a forger of art masterpieces would have given his artistic eye to duplicate. The place might have been crane-lifted from Rome and lowered square into the American Midwest with not so much as a brick lost.

After we exchanged greetings, I asked Seth about his recent lapses. He scowled, sighting along the edge of a drawer he was sanding.

"I said I forget things sometimes. And I didn't see June when I passed her on the street. These here glasses are for close work. Sometimes I don't get around to taking them off. I bet even the President does that now and again."

"One case of diminished capacity at a time, please," I said. "Why'd you turn down Scott's offer?"

"Didn't want to sell. I said that." He blew sawdust off the drawer.

"It's a lot of money. You could buy a chain of shops and still take a trip around the world."

"I like it here."

"That's not good enough. This is a money-driven society. It's going to look bad at the hearing when they ask you why you said no and that's the only answer you have."

Seth slid the drawer into place—it fit perfectly, of course—and straightened.

"My father built this shop with his own two hands. I been working in it sixty years. There's still some things you can't buy."

"That's it?"

"That's the truth. I can't put no varnish on it that would make it better."

I let it go for the time being. Everybody lies to his lawyer.

"Will you submit to a psychiatric examination?" Before he could protest I said, "I've a friend, Dr. Casper Fyfe, whom I've worked with before. He's good."

Seth swapped out his spectacles for a pair of safety glasses and picked up an electric sander. "Do what feels right."

He plugged in the sander, driving me out with the noise.

• • •

"Brace yourself." Fred Petrillo sounded smug over the telephone. "Two years ago, controlling interest in Scott Developments was snapped up by Global Enterprises."

I replaced the receiver. I don't remember if I thanked him; I was in shock.

Global Enterprises was a subsidiary of that organization with a five-letter name beginning with an *M* we're not supposed to talk about any more. It represented the organization's push to crack legitimate business, but from the number of vice-presidents who had shown up in automobile trunks at airports recently, it was clear that tactics hadn't changed since Prohibition. I filed the knowledge away for possible use later. At the time I had no reason to believe I'd need it soon.

Sharon showed Casper Fyfe in two days later. Grinning at her over the remains of my family-sized pizza, I folded the cardboard, chucked it into the wastebasket, and grasped Casper's hand. She glared back and closed the door harder than necessary on the way out. Sharon was a fitness freak.

"You aren't losing any weight." Casper sat down.

"I grow fat in the saddle, like Napoleon. What you got?"

"You won't like it." Lanky and balding, the psychiatrist wore the obligatory hornrims and had a square jaw that must have offered a tempting target during his college boxing days. "In this doctor's opinion, Seth Borden is something less than stable."

"We should both be so crazy."

"I'm serious, Matt. You know I don't joke about my work."

My heart dropped a notch. "Give me the details."

"It isn't senility. To put it in layman's terms, he suffered a trauma somewhere in his past that drove him permanently off center. If I had a couple of years I could probably find it, but that won't help you."

"Just how screwy is he?"

"Psychiatrists don't recognize that term," he chided. "There's enough abnormality to provide Scott's attorney with plenty of ammunition. His heart's not too good either, my stethoscope tells me, but that's beside the point. Any testimony I gave would do your case more harm than good."

"You think it will affect the judge's decision?"

"I don't know. It's an informal hearing, and Morton's presiding. He's emotional. Maybe a plot by the mob to gain a foothold in Roseacre will sway him our way, but you're the expert on that."

Casper recommended a psychiatrist to refute the generalities advanced by the state shrink; after which we parted company. I dialed Fred Petrillo at the capital for documentation to back up my forthcoming disclosure. The newspapers were going to fall in love with me.

The hearing went as I'd expected. Scott's lawyer scored points with the psychiatric testimony based on three visits with Seth Borden, a few of which I was able to knock down despite the handicap of my own expert's never having met the subject. I introduced Seth's ledger and balance sheets by way of showing that he was capable of operating his business. Judge Morton seemed unimpressed. At that point I'd hoped to present character witnesses who could swear to the old man's stability, but it turned out he had no close friends. Scott's man rested his case. Then I brought out the big guns.

News that organized crime had its eye on Roseacre played hell with decorum. Spectators babbled; Scott leapt to his feet, cursing me. A photographer burst a flashbulb in my face. Morton's gavel handle cracked while he was pounding. I rested my case. The hearing was recessed until the afternoon.

When it convened again, Seth was absent. Scrubbed and wearing an old suit frayed at the cuffs, he'd left after the morning session, muttering something about work do to. I sent Johnny, my best gofer, to the old man's shop to find out what was keeping him. After twenty minutes the boy returned, alone and white-faced. He whispered in my ear.

I rose. Morton's ice-blue eyes impaled me.

"Your honor, I've just learned that my client, Seth Borden, is dead."

June Scott gasped. Then the tears came.

Her husband put an arm around her awkwardly. The gallery buzzed.

"He was found collapsed on the floor of his shop moments ago," I continued. "A doctor is there now. It looks as if Mr. Borden suffered a heart attack—brought on, perhaps, by the strain of this morning's proceedings."

Judge Morton adjourned the court.

Public outcry was fierce when June Scott acquired the building from probate, but since an autopsy definitely established natural causes in the old man's death and no criminal acts could be traced directly to Global Enterprises, the law withdrew. June lost no time in ceding the property over to Global.

The day the shop was set to come down, Sharon put through a call from C. Burton Scott. He sounded upset.

"Meet me there, shyster." The receiver clicked in my ear.

The site was right around the corner from my office; but then most things are, in our little town. I found Scott in a hardhat and shiny blue suit standing outside a fence erected to keep out gawkers. His face was taut and pale. He seized my arm and steered me through the gate into the gutted shell of Seth's shop.

The wrecking crew had carted away everything worth salvaging, then gone to work with sledgehammers and crowbars. I was dragged stumbling over bricks and broken mortar, past hardhatted workers standing around idle, to a gaping hole in the south wall. Scott let go of me to snatch a flashlight out of an employee's hand, switched it on. The hard white beam lanced the darkness inside the cavity.

I can't say I was surprised. The trauma in Seth's past, the extensive remodeling, his unwillingness to sell when he knew it would mean the shop's destruction, formed a pattern I had worked with often. I hadn't said anything because there was nothing to be gained by doing so. That cost me trouble with the police later.

Dental records confirmed it after two days, but from the start there was no doubt that the broken skeleton lying crumpled in one corner of the ruined wall belonged to Bedelia Borden, Seth's money-mad sister, dead these twenty years.

# Saturday Night at the Mikado Massage

*I'm partial to underdog stories; who isn't? I enjoyed researching this one.*

The ironic thing about the night Mr. Ten Fifty-Five died on Iiko's table was that she was supposed to have that Saturday off.

She'd asked for the time three weeks in advance so she could spend the weekend with Uncle Trinh, who was coming to visit from Corpus Christi, Texas, where he worked on a shrimp boat, but the day before his bus left, he slipped on some fish scales and broke his leg. Now he needed money for doctors' bills, and Iiko had volunteered to work.

The Mikado Massage was located on Michigan Avenue in Detroit. On one side was an empty building that had once sheltered a travel agency. The Mystic Arts Bookshop was on the other and shared a common wall with the Mikado. There was a fire door in this wall, which came in handy during election years. When the mayor sent police with warrants, they invariably found the bookshop full of customers and the massage parlor empty. On the third Sunday of every month a man came to collect for the service of keeping the owner informed about these visits. Iiko had seen the man's picture under some printing on the side of a van with a loudspeaker on the roof. Detroit was the same as back home except for no Ho Chi Minh on the billboards.

Although its display in the Yellow Pages advertised an all-Japanese staff, the Mikado's owner, Mr. Shigeta, was the only person in residence not Korean or Vietnamese, and he was never seen by the customers unless one of them became ungallant. He was a short, thick man of fifty-five or seventy with hair exactly like a seal's, who claimed to have stood in for Harold Sakata on the set of *Goldfinger* and had papered his little office with posters and lobby cards from the film. One of them was supposed to have been signed by Sean Connery, but when Iiko began to learn to read English she saw that Sean was misspelled.

She had been working there four months. She made less than the other masseuses because she was still on probation after a police visit to the Dragon's Gate in the suburb of Inkster, which had no fire door, and so she gave only massages, no specials. She kept track of the two months remaining on her sentence on a Philgas calendar inside her locker door.

The man she called Mr. Ten Fifty-Five always showed up at that time on Saturday night and always asked for Iiko. Because he reminded her a little of Uncle Trinh, she'd thought to do him a kindness and had explained to him, in her imperfect English, that he could get the same massage for much less at any hotel, but he said he preferred the Mikado. The hotels didn't offer Japanese music or heated floors or scented oils or a pink bulb in a table lamp with a paper kimono shade.

Normally, Saturday was the busiest night of the week, but this was the Saturday after Thanksgiving, when, as Mr. Shigeta explained, the customers remembered they were family men and stayed home. Mr. Ten Fifty-Five, therefore, was the only person she'd seen since early evening when Mr. Shigeta had gone home, leaving her in charge.

Mr. Ten Fifty-Five was duck-shaped and bald, with funny gray tufts that stood out on both sides of his head when he waddled in from the shower in a towel and sprawled facedown on the table. He often fell asleep the moment she began to rub him down and didn't wake up even when she walked on his back, so it wasn't until she asked him to turn over that Iiko found out that this time he'd died.

Iiko recognized death. She'd been only a baby when the last American soldier left her village, but she remembered the marauding gangs that swept through after the Fall of Saigon, claiming to be hunting rebels but forcing themselves upon the women and carrying away tins of food and silver picture frames and setting the buildings on fire when they left. Iiko's brother Nguyen, sixteen years old, had tried to block the door of their parents' home, but one of the visitors stuck a bayonet between his ribs and planted a boot on his face to tug loose the blade. Iiko hung on to her mother's skirt during the walk to the cemetery. The skirt was white, the color of mourning in Vietnam, with a border of faded flowers at the hem.

When Iiko confirmed that Mr. Ten Fifty-Five's heart had stopped, she went through his clothes. This was much easier than picking pockets in Ho Chi Minh City, where one always ran the risk of being caught with one's hand in the pocket of another pickpocket. Iiko found car keys, a little plastic bottle two-thirds full of tiny white pills, a tattered billfold containing fifty-two dollars, and a folding knife with a stag handle and a blade that had been ground down to a quarter-inch wide. She placed it and the money in the pocket of her smock and returned the clothes to the back of the chair. The tail of the shabby coat clunked when it flapped against a chair leg.

Iiko investigated. There was a lump at the bottom where the machine stitch that secured the lining had been replaced by a clumsy crosshatch of thread that didn't match the original. This came loose easily, and she removed a small green cloth sack with a drawstring, whose contents caught the pink light in seven spots of reflected purple. When she switched on the overhead bulb, the stones, irregular ovals the size of the charcoal bits she swept weekly from the brazier in the sauna, turned deep blue.

She found a place for the stones, then went out into the little reception area to call Mr. Shigeta at home. He would want to know that a customer had died so that when the police came they would find nothing of interest except a dead customer. While she was dialing, two men came in.

Both were Americans. One, a large black man with a face that was all jutting bones, wore jeans, a sweatshirt, and a Pistons jacket. He towered over his companion, a white man with small features and sandy hair done up elaborately, wearing a shiny black suit with a pinched waist and jagged lapels. Their eyes continued to move after the men had come to a stop a few feet from the counter, searching the room.

"Sorry, we close," Iiko said.

She was standing in front of the sign that said OPEN TILL MIDNIGHT.

"You're back open," said the sandy-haired man. "Long enough anyway to tell us where's the fat bulb guy that came in here about eleven."

She shook her head, indicating that she didn't understand. It was not entirely a lie. The sandy-haired man, who did almost all the talking, spoke very fast.

"Come on, girlie, we know he's here. His car's outside."

"The stuff ain't in it, neither," said the black man.

"Shut up, Leon."

"Not know," said Iiko.

"Leon."

The black man put a hand inside his jacket and brought out a big silver gun with a twelve-inch barrel. He pointed it at her and thumbed back the hammer.

The sandy man said, "Leon's killed three men and a woman, but he's never to my knowledge done a slant. Where's George?"

"Not know George," she said.

"Keep it on her. If she jumps, take off her head." The sandy man came around the counter.

Iiko stood still while the man ran his hands over her smock. She didn't move even when they lingered at her small breasts and crotch. He took the fifty-two dollars and the knife from her pockets. He showed Leon the knife.

"That's George's shank, all right," said the black man. "He carries it open when he has to walk more'n a block to his car. He's almost as scared of muggers as he is of guns."

The sandy man slapped Iiko's face. She remained unmoving. She could feel the hot imprint of his palm on her cheek.

"One more time before we disturb the peace, Dragon Lady. Where's George Myrtle?"

She turned and went through the door behind the counter. The two men followed.

In the massage room the sandy man felt behind Mr. Ten Fifty-Five's ear, then said, "Deader'n Old Yeller."

"I don't see no marks," Leon said.

"Of course not. Look at him. He as good as squiffed himself the day he topped two forty and started taking elevators instead of climbing the stairs. I bet he never said no to a pork chop in his life. Check out his clothes."

Leon returned the big gun to a holster under his left arm and quickly turned out all the pockets of the coat and trousers, then with a grunt held the coat upside down and showed his companion the place where the lining had been pulled loose.

The sandy man looked at Iiko. She saw something in his pale eyes that she remembered from the day her brother was killed.

"This ain't turning out like I figured," the sandy man said. "I was looking forward to watching Leon bat around that tub of guts till he told us what he done with them hot rocks. I sure don't enjoy watching him do that to a woman. Especially not to a pretty little China doll like you. How's about sparing me that unpleasantness and telling me what you did with the merch?"

"Not know merch," she said truthfully.

Leon started toward her. The sandy man stopped him with a hand. He was still looking at Iiko.

"You got more of these rooms?" he asked.

After a moment she nodded and stepped in the direction of the curtain over the doorway. The black man's bulk blocked that path.

"Search the rest of the place, Leon. I'll take care of this."

"Sure?"

"Sure."

Leon went out. Iiko led the sandy man through the curtains and across the narrow hallway. This room was larger, although still small. A forest of bottles containing scented oils stood on a rack beside the massage table. The sandy man seized her arm and spun her around. They were close now, and the light in his eyes had changed. She could smell his aftershave, sticky and sharp.

"You're sure a nice little piece for a slant. I bet old George had some times with you. Especially at the end. It's gonna take the undertaker a week to pry that grin off his face."

Iiko didn't struggle.

The sandy man said, "I could use a little rub myself. You rub me, I rub you. What do you say? Then we'll talk."

After a moment she nodded. "Take off clothes."

"You first."

He let go of her and stepped back, his small, hard fists dangling at his sides. He watched her unbutton and peel off the smock. Without hesitating, she undid her halter top and stepped out of her shorts. She wore no underthings. She knew her body was good, firm and well-proportioned for her small frame. She could see in his eyes he approved.

He took a long breath and let it out. Then he took off his shiny black coat. He hung his suit carefully on the wooden hanger on the wall peg, folded his shirt, and put it on the seat of the chair. His ribs showed, but his pale, naked arms and legs were sinewy, the limbs of a runner.

He saw that she saw. "I work out. I ain't going to do you no favor like George and clock out on the table."

She said nothing. He stretched out on his stomach on the padded table. "No oil," he said. "I don't want to ruin my clothes. Just powder."

She reached for the can of talcum. While her back was turned to him, she laid down the folding knife she had removed from the sandy man's pocket while he was holding her, poking it behind a row of bottles.

She sprinkled the powder on his back, set down the can, and worked her hands along his spine and scapula. His muscles jumped and twitched beneath her palms, not at all like the loose, unresisting flesh of Mr. Ten Fifty-Five. She had the impression the sandy man was poised to leap off the table at the first sign of suspicious behavior. She heard glass breaking in another part of the building as Leon continued his search for the blue stones.

Iiko was a skilled masseuse. Unlike some of her fellow employees, who merely went through the motions until the big moment when they asked the customers to turn over, Iiko had been trained by a licensed massage therapist. She flattered herself that she still managed to give satisfaction even under the strictures of probation. Gradually she felt the sandy man's body relax beneath her expert hands.

To maintain contact, she kept one palm on his lower spine while with the other she retrieved the knife from its hiding place on the rack of bottles, pried it open with her teeth, and with one swift underhand motion jammed the blade into his back as far as it would go and dragged it around his right kidney as if she were coring an apple. The sandy man made very little noise dying.

When the body had ceased to shudder, she dressed and left the room. She'd dropped the knife; she'd come to regret that. The sound of a heavy piece of furniture scraping across a wooden floor told her that Leon was moving the desk in Mr. Shigeta's office. The way to the front door and out led directly past that room; she did not want to take the chance of running into the black man as he came out. She let herself into the Mystic Arts Bookshop by way of the fire door in the wall that separated the two establishments.

The shop had been closed for hours. She groped her way through darkness to the front door but found that exit barred by a deadbolt lock that required a key. The same was true of the back door. An ornamental grid sealed the windows. For a moment Iiko stood still and waited for her thoughts to settle. There was a telephone on the counter, she knew; but that must wait. However much time she'd bought must be invested in action. It would not be long before Leon discovered the sandy man's body, and then he would find the fire door. The lock was on the massage parlor side.

She switched on a light. Tall racks of musty-smelling books divided the room into narrow aisles. She removed a heavy dictionary from the reference section, carried it to the common wall, and set the book on the floor in front of the steel door. She repeated the procedure with another large book and then another. At the end of ten minutes she had erected a formidable barrier. Then she lifted the telephone.

She jumped when the thumb latch went down, stood and backed away from instinct when the door moved a fraction of an inch and stopped, impeded by the stacked books. She dialed 911, and when the operator asked what was her emergency, she laid the receiver on its side facing the fire door.

Just then Leon pushed the door hard. Two of the stacks fell, creating an avalanche. A pause, and then the black man gave a lunge. More books tumbled, but now the pile was wedged between the door and a metal rack weighted down with scores of books. It would not budge another inch.

Iiko switched off the light. A bank of deep shadow appeared on the side of the fire door nearest the latch, and she slipped into it noiselessly. She was just inches away from the black man. He'd worked up a sweat searching the Mikado for the missing stones and wrestling with the door; she could smell the clean sharp sting of it.

Nothing stirred in the bookshop. She heard the black man's heavy breathing as he paused to gather strength, heard the buzzing queries of the 911 operator coming through the earpiece of the telephone a dozen steps away.

With an explosive grunt, Leon threw all his weight against the door. The pile of books crumpled against the base of the rack, the covers bending.

Another pause, this one shorter. Two hundred pounds of solid muscle struck the door with the force of a battering ram. The rack teetered, tilted, hung at a twenty-degree angle for an impossible length of time; then it toppled. Books plummeted from its shelves; steel struck the floor with a bang that shook the building. To the operator listening at police headquarters it must have sounded like an artillery barrage. Leon thrust his arm and shoulder through the gap. The big silver gun made the arm look ridiculously long. His entire body seemed to swell with the effort to squeeze past the edge of the door. Now would have been a good time to have that knife Iiko had left behind, but her life had taught her that regrets were time wasted for a life that was already short. He grunted again, and the noise turned into a howl of triumph as he stumbled into the bookshop.

But his eyes were unaccustomed to the darkness, and he set his foot on a spilled stack of books that turned under his weight. He sprawled headlong across the pile.

The opening into the massage parlor was more than wide enough for Iiko. She darted through, and before Leon could get to his feet, she seized the door handle and yanked it shut behind her, flicking the lock button with her thumb.

In the next minute it didn't matter that the 911 operator could hear the black man pounding the steel door with his fists. The air was shrill with sirens, red and blue strobes throbbed through the windows of the Mikado. Gravel pelted the side of the building as police cruisers skidded around the corner into the parking lot of the Mystic Arts.

Iiko did not pay much attention to the bullhorn-distorted demands for surrender next door, or even the rattle of gunfire when Leon, exhausted and confused by the turn of events since he and the sandy man had entered the Mikado, burst a lock and plunged out into the searchlights with the big silver gun in his hand. She was busy with the narrow metal dustpan she used to clean out the brazier in the sauna, sifting through the smoldering bits of charcoal in the bottom. The stones were covered with soot and difficult to distinguish from the coals, but when she washed them in the sink they shone with the same icy blueness that had caught her eye in the massage room.

The glowing coals had burned away the green cloth bag as she'd known they would. She wrapped the stones carefully in a flannel facecloth, put the bundle in the side pocket of the cloth coat she drew on over her smock, and started toward the front door. Then she remembered the fifty-two dollars the sandy man had taken from her and put in the pocket of his shiny black suit.

The sandy man was as she'd left him, naked and dead, only paler than before. She thrust the money into her other side pocket and went out.

Waiting at the corner for the bus, Iiko thought she would take the stones to the pawnshop man who bought the jewelry and gold money clips she managed from time to time to take from the clothing of her customers. The pawnshop man knew many people and had always dealt with her honestly. She hoped the stones would sell for enough to settle some of Uncle Trinh's doctors' bills.

# How's My Driving?

*My dad would have liked this one, I think; he drove a big rig twenty years and belonged to Teamsters Local 299 in Detroit, when Jimmy Hoffa ran it before stepping up to assume the national presidency. If you disparaged Jimmy in front of my old man, you'd have lived to regret it.*

The truck stop was lit up like a Hollywood movie premiere, an oval of incandescence in an undeveloped landscape where a county road ducked under the interstate. I parked my rig in the football field–sized lot and went into the diner, a little unsteady on my pins. I'd been stuck for an hour in a snarl caused by someone's broken axle and a thousand cars slowing down to gape at it, and I'd hit the flask a few times to flatten my nerves. If I missed my contact tonight it would be another week before he came back the other direction.

Brooks & Dunn were whining on the retro-look juke as I took a stool at the end of the counter. Most of the other customers were seated in booths. I counted eleven, shoveling out their plates and blowing steam off their thick mugs. It was late and there was a lull between early escapees from the traffic jam and the next batch backed up at the scales. The waitress, a tired-looking blonde of forty or so, came over with a clean mug and a carafe. In those places they put coffee in front of you the way they do a glass of water in others.

I nodded at the question on her face and watched her pour. "I bet you hate these slow times," I said.

She was silent for a moment, looking at me, and I knew I was being sized up for a pickup artist or just friendly. "I don't know which is worse," she said then, "this or the rush. When it's on I need six hands to keep up and when it isn't I don't know what to do with the two I've got."

"My old man said he'd rather work than wait." I sipped. She made a pretty good pot. There's a trick to brewing strong coffee without making it bitter.

"He a trucker too?"

"He was a hood. They've got him doing ninety-nine years and a day in Joliet for murder."

"Well, there's a conversation starter I don't hear every night." But I could tell she didn't believe me.

I didn't try to set her straight. The whiskey had loosened me up too much. I needed to put something on top of it. "You serve breakfast all the time?"

She said sure, it's a truck stop, and I ordered scrambled and a ham steak. She gave it to the cook through the pass-through to the kitchen without writing it down and left the counter to fresh the other customers' coffee. When she got back she served me and refilled my cup. She watched me eat.

"You seem pretty well-adjusted for the son of a convict."

"I was grown when he went in," I said, chewing. "It wasn't his first time, though. He did two separate bits for manslaughter on plea deals. Cops figured him for at least fifteen, but they only got him good on the last one."

She hoisted her eyebrows. "He was a serial killer?"

"Hell, no. Serial killers are loonies who slept with their mothers. He was a pro."

"A hit man? Like for the mob?"

"Most of the time. Sometimes he freelanced, but you can get jammed up working for civilians. I wouldn't touch one of those." I realized what I'd said and changed the subject in a hurry. "Got any more hash browns?"

She put in the order. A trucker came in, one of the sloppy ones with a belly and tobacco stains in the corners of his mouth, and sat down at the other end of the counter. She ordered him a burger and a Coke and came back with the hash browns. "You've got a real line of crap, but it's one I never heard. So how'd the cops trip him up?"

"Circumstantial evidence. He ran a bar in Jersey, and guys kept going in and never coming out. His lawyer objected, but the judge was a hardcase and allowed it in. There was some other stuff, but the past history's what clinched it for the jury." I poured ketchup on the potatoes. "That was his mistake, always operating in the same place. The best way to avoid drawing suspicion is to move around a lot: one hit in Buffalo, the next in Kansas City, another in Seattle. Get yourself a front that involves plenty of travel."

"Like truck driving."

I took a long draft of coffee. I was going to have to change my brand of booze. The one I drank talked and talked.

"Sure. Or sales. The bigger the territory, the less chance of the cops getting together and comparing notes. Anyway, that's how I'd do it."

"Trucking's better," she said. "No one looks twice. You all run to the same type."

I turned my head to look at Big Belly waiting for his hamburger. Then I grinned at her.

"Okay," she said, "two types. One looks like a pro wrestler gone to seed, the other like Randy Travis. The point is there's a lot of both. Traveling salesmen are about extinct. You notice the ones that are left." She folded her arms and leaned them on the counter. There were circles under her eyes and she was older than I liked them in general, but she had good cheekbones and serious eyes. I'd had my fill of the playful kind. "How do you work it? Do they call you or do you check in?"

Just then the cook set the burger and a plate of slimy fries on the sill. She delivered them without comment and took up the same position at my end, arms folded on the counter.

I pushed away my plates, unrolled the pack from my sleeve, and held it up. A NO SMOKING sign hung in plain sight on the wall behind her, but she shrugged. I got out two, gave her one, and lit them both. "If I went in for that work," I said, blowing smoke, "I'd have them call that eight-hundred number on the back of my truck. You know the one."

She nodded. "'How's My Driving?' with the number to call and complain. I can't remember the last time I saw a truck that didn't have it."

"That's what's beautiful about it. I'd have it forwarded to my cell. If I cut someone off in traffic and he called, I'd tell him I'd look into it, blow him off, like I'm a dispatcher. The other kind, the paying kind, if the cops trace it I can always say it was a wrong number. If there were no complications I'd adjust my route and take care of business."

"Pretty smart."

"Smarter than my old man, anyway. Smart enough not to go in for that line of work."

She straightened up and put out her cigarette in what was left of my eggs. "I thought so. Just another pickup. The trouble with you guys is you've seen *Bonnie and Clyde* one too many times. You think every girl who slings hash is just waiting for her chance to hook up with some road-show Jesse James."

"*Badlands*, actually. But you've got me pegged."

She figured my bill, slapped it on the counter, and left to bus tables. I finished my cigarette and paid, leaving fifteen percent. I wanted to leave more, but I'd done too much already to make her remember me. I went back out to my rig.

It's a nice one, a secondhand Freightliner with an orange tractor and a shiny silver trailer; when new it had set someone back the price of a house on the beach. In the sleeping quarters behind the seat I switched on the light, went over my notes one more time and looked at the driver's license photo blowup and telephoto candids once again for luck, then fed them to the cross-shredder I'd added to the standard equipment. I looked at my watch. I had better than an hour to kill. His company had him on a tight schedule, and he couldn't afford to lose another job. The feds had told him he had no more coming if he expected any more help from them.

Twenty to midnight. I took two more hits from the flask and went back into the diner.

Big Belly had finished his meal and left. I waited while she rang up a middle-aged tourist couple with fanny packs, then asked if she got off at midnight.

"Why? You going to buy me a cuppa and tell me you're an international spy?"

"I started off on the wrong foot. I'll make it cappuccino if it'll make up for being a jerk."

She thought that over. She frowned more attractively than most women smiled. I had an almost overpowering urge to see what her smile looked like. She was as hard to put away as the flask, which I had now in my hip pocket.

"I'm on till four," she said. "But I'm past due for a break. Coffee's fine, but I wouldn't mind a slice of pie."

She asked the cook to cover the counter and brought the coffees and a wedge of lemon meringue to a booth in the smoking section, away from the others. I produced the flask and when she nodded I trickled some of it into both cups. We tapped them together in an unspoken toast.

She made a face when she tasted it. "I suppose it's good whiskey, but you don't drink it in coffee for the taste, do you?"

"My old man only drank it this way when he had a cold."

"You're not going to talk about him again, are you?"

"That subject's closed."

We shared small talk, or what passed for it between strangers late at night. Her name was Elizabeth; she preferred Beth, but she had *Liz* scripted on her uniform blouse and said I could call her that as long as she was dressed for this job. She was working two jobs to earn enough to pay a lawyer to get custody of her ten-year-old daughter. She was a recovering meth addict. Her lawyer said if she could stay clean for another six months she had a better chance in court. "So much for budding romance," she said, forking pie into her mouth.

"If I go on hitting the stuff the way I've been lately, we'll both be in the same boat." I added more to my cup. She frowned again when I offered to freshen hers, then nodded. The coffee was still hot; the fumes entered my nose and speeded up the process. I had to close one eye to see only one of her.

"Conscience," she said. "I guess you have to anesthetize yourself to make a clean job of it."

I couldn't tell if she was needling me or if she was really interested. I asked her what her other job was.

"Not as glamorous as this. Tell me about some of the people you've killed."

I looked at her, closing one eye. Her mouth twitched at the corners. It was going to be one of those conversations. In the same vein I told her about Omaha and then Sioux Falls, that bitched-up job that had almost got me pinched. I'd spent a nervous day maneuvering myself back into position to make it good. I was careful to speak hypothetically, spinning a story to keep the lady's interest.

I put away the flask, but by then I wasn't paying as much attention as I should have. I told her what I was working on, an open contract; a hundred and fifty grand to the man who made an example of a mouthy errand boy who'd blabbed enough in court to take down a chunk of the East Coast and put him in the Witness Protection Program. But Anderson was a grifter who couldn't resist the temptation to turn a dishonest dollar even if it brought attention and he had to be relocated under yet another identity. At present he was delivering office furniture from Cincinnati to L.A. and back, with a new face courtesy of the taxpayers to keep him from being recognized in case of a chance encounter with a former acquaintance. I'd started out careful, but somewhere along the way

I stopped being hypothetical and mentioned the fact that Anderson always put in at that truck stop and was due there in a little while.

"Do you use a gun?"

"I have, but it makes a lot of noise. A knife's better for close work, and you know right away if you made it good. Also it's cheaper to replace when you leave it at the scene, with the prints wiped off, and you don't get jammed up if the cops find one on you. A lot of truckers carry buck knives for quick repairs."

I heard myself then, and it sobered me up in a hurry. Then she chuckled, shaking her head, and the smile turned out to have been worth waiting for.

"You sure do sling the bull." She finished her pie and slid away the plate. "I ought to dump my coffee in your lap. So why am I not doing that?"

I took out my pack and lit us both, relieved. "Maybe I'm the first guy you ever met in this place didn't think pushing a rig was the most romantic job in America. It's boring as hell is what it is. You make up stories just to keep from aiming straight at a bridge abutment."

"It's pretty clever, especially that bit about being able to move around being a big advantage. You ought to write for the movies."

"You need to know somebody," I said. "And it helps to know how to spell."

She laughed. I grinned. It was going to be all right. Then the cook made a racket behind the counter and that meant her break was over. She thanked me for the pie and the entertainment and I got up like a gentleman when she rose. She pressed against me briefly; probably an accident, but try telling that to my physical reaction. I was going to have to stop in on my way back across country.

Back behind the wheel I stuck the flask in the glove compartment and fired up the diesel. The Anderson job was out, at least at that location. If I was to get a jump on all the others looking for a big payday I'd have to follow him when he left, run him off some lonely section of road, and do the job with a jack handle, or anything but a knife. It would help that he wasn't going by the name Anderson and that the feds would make sure it didn't get out that a witness in their care came to a bad end. If Liz read about it, she'd think it was an accident and wouldn't connect it with me.

One thing was sure. I needed to save the whiskey from then on for after the job, as a treat instead of a stimulus to action.

Anderson pulled up half an hour late, his company rig plastered with mud from some detour down a dirt road, probably in search of a craps game. The man had no pride, in his workmanship or anything else. The cargo of Arrow shirts I was carrying may have been just a cover, but I'd deliver them on time. Apart from ridding the world of a rotten snitch, I'd be doing some dispatcher the favor of not having to can him.

He went into the diner, looking as sloppy as the way he approached his duties. I remembered what Liz had said about there being two types of truck, the big-bellied kind and the kind that looked like Randy Travis. I adjusted the rearview for a look at the stalwart chin, the granite squint, the hair cut short at the temples and left long in front to tumble go-to-hell fashion over the forehead. She'd felt firm and warm pressing against me. I wanted another pull at the flask but I tamped down the temptation with a smoke.

I dozed off, I think. I jumped, alert all at once and cursing, but Anderson's filthy tractor-trailer stood where he'd left it and the clock on the dash told me only five minutes had passed. At least I'd had the presence of mind to ditch the butt in the ashtray, where it had smoked itself out. I didn't remember doing it. Blackouts are a good sign to cut back.

I turned on a late-night talk show for company: the war, the economy, yet another scandal on Capitol Hill. If I'd ever had reason to regret the path my life had taken, self-esteem was only a dial switch away. I put in Johnny Cash and tried to keep up with him on the Rock Island Line.

Forty minutes passed, an hour. I pictured Anderson lingering over a plate of slop, maybe chatting up Liz. I hoped to hell he wasn't trying to impress her with his career in crime.

I got restless after ninety minutes. His desks and crap were due in Milwaukee by noon. I didn't picture him highballing it to make his deadline. He was exceeding even the margin of ineptitude I'd drawn up for him. I ditched the cigarette I'd started and stepped down to investigate. He didn't know me from Donald Duck. I could sit slurping coffee on the stool next to his and he'd think I was just another gear-cruncher, feeling all superior because he was just slumming from the wise-guy life.

The place was jumping. Just in the time I'd been out of the loop the lot had filled with Macks and Peterbilts and the odd Winnebago, and Liz was too busy filling mugs and plunking down bowls of chili to notice me. There were more beer guts than Travises crowding the counter, but Anderson wasn't among them, nor at any of the booths, where the knights of the road sat belching onions and air-shifting down steep mountain grades for their bored audiences. I went down the narrow tiled corridor that led to the showers and toilets.

Anderson wasn't in any of them, not even the ladies' room, where a schnook like him might wander into without stopping to read the sign on the door.

The only door left was marked EMPLOYEES ONLY.

He lay there on the floor among the mops and cartons of toilet paper and industrial-sized mustard dispensers, on his face in the middle of a stain that didn't look like anything but what it was. I bent to feel his neck for a pulse, but didn't get that far. The knife stuck out hilt-deep from just below his shoulder blade, flat, with a brass heel and a printed woodgrain on the steel handle. I groped for the buck knife in my left pants pocket, purely from reflex. It wasn't there.

The door flew open and the rest was shouting and shoving and my feet kicked out from under me and two hundred pounds of county law kneeling on my back and the muzzle of a big sidearm tickling the back of my neck. I heard my rights and felt my shoulders pulled almost out of their sockets and the cold hard heavy clamp of the cuffs on my wrists.

I kept my mouth shut, credit me that. I was as sober as a Shaker, and met every pair of eyes that locked with mine during the hustle through the crowded diner and out the door toward the radio car, where some kind of soul who cared whether I suffered a concussion pressed down my head with an iron palm, shoved me into the back seat, and slammed the door.

The lot was desert-bright, sheriff's spotlights adding candlepower to the pole lamps, the night air throbbing with sirens grinding down and radios muttering and spectators' chatter and the monotonous drone of official voices ordering the crowd to disperse, go home to your families, nothing to see here. I sat staring at the gridded polyurethane sheet that separated me from the front seat, where a fullback in uniform sat on one haunch with a foot on the pavement, murmuring into a mike, lights twinkling on the Christmas-tree console that divided the bucket seats in front.

When I got tired of looking at that I stared at the carpeted floor at my feet. I hadn't a chance with a not-guilty plea. The cops would track me through the ICC log and place me at the scene of every hit I'd performed. A good prosecutor would find a way to bring that out in court, even if my knife in Anderson's back wasn't enough. ("Someone picked your pocket? *That's* your defense?") You can't argue with the record. I was pinned as tightly as my old man in his bar, where customers kept going in and never came out.

I raised my eyes to meet those of the curious pressing in for a closer look, before they were manhandled out of the way by the hard men who had taken over the truck stop. One of the pairs of eyes belonged to Liz, looking less tired now, with that smile on her face as she made a gun with her finger and shot me with it.

I didn't know what it meant at first. Our conversation had taken place on the other side of the flask and came drifting back in pieces. One piece slowed down long enough for me to reel in.

*Her other job wasn't as glamorous as this.*

And as she faded back into the crowd, I heard the rest, as clearly as if she were still speaking: "You don't have to move around. I see just as many opportunities as you do just staying in one place."

# The Pioneer Strain

*This was my second published short story. Even when I was young, I felt a closer bond to members of the generation ahead of mine than my own. I know Molly Dodd better than some close friends of my youth. (I came up with the name years before TV introduced* The Days and Nights of Molly Dodd, *a character who bore no resemblance to mine.)*

"A rifle!" Vernon Thickett stared up at his fellow deputy from behind a steaming hot bowl of Maud Baxter's notorious Red River Chili and cursed.

Earl Briggs nodded. He was a lean country boy, leaner even than Thickett, and with his shock of untrained wheat-colored hair and freckle-spattered face he looked far too young to be wearing a star on his buff shirt. "That's what I said, Verne. She's got a rifle and Lord knows how many cartridges up there and she threatened to blow a hole in her nephew's nice tailor-made suit if he didn't clear off her land."

"Did he take her advice?"

A quick grin flashed across the younger deputy's face. "You know Leroy, Verne. What do you think?"

"I think he took her advice. Where is he now?"

"Out on Route Forty-four. He called the office from one of those free telephones the highway department put in last spring."

"Madder'n a half-squashed bee, I expect." Thickett made a face at his untouched meal and pushed himself to his feet. He towered over Earl by a head. "Get in touch with Luke and Dan and tell 'em to get over to Molly's place on the double and wait for me. No sirens. We don't want any state troopers in on this one. Then bring my car around in front of the office while I grab a gun. That's the only thing the old girl understands." When Earl had left to carry out his orders Thickett snatched a slice of bread from the table, spooned a quantity of chili onto it, slapped another slice on top of that and, nodding to hefty Maud Baxter behind the counter, strode toward the door of the diner with the sandwich in his mouth.

He didn't say a word to Earl all the way out to Molly's place. Verne Thickett was not the law in Schuylerville, Oklahoma, but as long as Sheriff Willis was in the hospital recuperating from a gall bladder operation he was the next best thing. Until now his biggest headache had been the kids who kept stealing the outhouse from behind Guy Dawson's place and hauling it up onto the roof of whatever schoolteacher happened to be the target of their hostilities that week. As for Molly Dodd, she was trouble enough at any time, but the kind of trouble she usually caused seldom involved the law. Molly Dodd armed with a rifle was one problem he wouldn't wish on his worst enemy.

For the past two years she and her nephew, Leroy Cooper, had been engaged in a bitter legal battle over the ownership of the 160 acres she lived on up in the Osage Hills. The Great Midwestern Bank and Trust Company, of which Leroy was the Schuylerville branch manager, claimed the land in lieu of payment on the loan it had made to Molly's late husband back in 1969, while she maintained that he had paid it off shortly before his death in 1973. Molly, now in her late seventies, had been part of Schuylerville for so long that most of the town had sided with her throughout the complex legal maneuvering, but that had come to an end three weeks before when the county court of appeals found in favor of the bank and issued an order for Molly Dodd's eviction.

Thickett berated himself for not anticipating the present situation. The pioneer strain in Molly was too strong to allow her to give in easily. He remembered the story his father had told of the time she'd come home early from a visit to find the house dark and her best friend's flivver parked in the driveway. Instead of going in and shooting Clyde and his lover—which, according to the moral code of the time, would have seemed the natural thing to do—she had simply climbed into the shiny new car, driven it into the next county, and sold it. The story had it that Clyde ended the affair soon afterward, and there was no record in the sheriff's office of a car being stolen that year. True or not, the account was worthy of Molly's reputation for audacity and ingenuity.

It was certainly a funnier story than the one currently unfolding up in the hills.

Leroy Cooper's sedan was parked at the side of the private road that led to the house at the top of the hill. A pair of scout cars were parked across from it at different angles. Earl ground the car to a dusty halt behind the civilian vehicle and they got out.

Cooper separated himself from the two deputies with whom he'd been conversing and came forward. "I want the woman arrested, Deputy! Do you know she actually threatened to shoot me? I barely got out of there with my life!"

"Take it easy, Leroy." Thickett slid his Stetson to the back of his head. "Do you mind telling me what you were doing up here in the first place?"

"I merely reminded her to vacate the premises before midnight tonight. That's the deadline set by the court. The bulldozers come in tomorrow."

"That's our job, Leroy. Why didn't you call us first?"

The banker looked as if Thickett had just asked him to scrub out a spittoon with his monogrammed shirt. "This is a family matter, Deputy. There seemed no reason to involve the law."

"It's a little late, isn't it?—What've we got, Luke?"

Luke Madden, the older of the two deputies already on the scene, was a big man with a bulldog jaw and hair the color of dull steel. He had been a deputy when Wilbur Underhill stormed through the area in 1933, and his prized possession was a framed newspaper clipping that described his inconclusive shoot-out with the outlaw. He spoke with a Blue Diamond matchstick clamped between his teeth. "That cabin's butted smack up against the side of the hill. There's only one way in or out by car, and this here's it. If you and Earl and Dan can keep her busy in front, Verne, I can sneak around the long way and take her from behind."

"How are you going to get in, through the chimney?" The chief deputy squinted up at the gabled structure atop the hill. "I reckon we'll just go on up and give her the chance to surrender."

The four-car caravan took off with Earl and Thickett in the lead and Leroy Cooper timidly bringing up the rear in his gleaming sedan. They were rounding the final turn before the house when a shot rang out and a bullet starred the windshield between the two deputies in front. Earl yanked the wheel hard to the right. The unmarked cruiser jumped the bank and came to a jarring stop in a bed of weeds at the side of the road. They both spilled out Thickett's side of the car and crouched there, guns drawn.

"Verne! Earl! You boys all right?" The voice was Luke Madden's, shouting from behind his car parked perpendicularly across the road. The way beyond it was completely blocked by the other two vehicles.

"We're fine!" Thickett shouted back. "Stay down!"

"She means business," said Earl. "Maybe I ought to radio the state troopers."

"No need. If Molly had meant to hit us, she'd have hit us. I've seen her pick nails off a fencepost at thirty yards. She's just trying to scare us."

"She's awful good at it."

No more shots came, and for a long time the only sound belonged to an occasional breeze whistling through the upper branches of the towering pines that surrounded the house on three sides. The house itself appeared deserted. All but one of the tall front windows were shaded. The one to the left of the front door was wide open. Five full minutes passed before a voice like a bull's bellow called out through the open window.

"You boys just get back into your automobiles and drive on out of here," it said. "I don't want to hurt nobody, but I will if I have to!"

Thickett cupped his hands around his mouth and shouted. "Molly, this here's Vernon Thickett! Put down that rifle and let us come in! You're not a criminal! Don't act like one!"

There was a short silence. Then, from the house: "I've knowed you since you was a baby, Vernon, and you know I don't want to harm you none! But you know I will if it means keepin' what's mine!"

"That's what I want to talk to you about, Molly! I—" Vernon had started to rise when another shot sounded, the bullet zinging along the roof of the unmarked scout car, missing his right ear by a couple of inches. He dove to the ground. "She hasn't lost a thing in the marksmanship department," he said to Earl. "This is going to take more than just words."

"You think?"

Six more reports came in rapid succession. Thickett turned his head as Luke Madden ran toward him in a crouch, bullets kicking up dirt at his heels. "Luke, what in *hell* do you think you're doing?" he demanded, when the older deputy was sprawled beside him, panting like an old hound-dog. "I told you to stay put!"

"Look!" Luke gasped for breath. "If I can get around to the other side of the hill without her seeing me, I can drop down onto the roof and climb in through one of them gabled windows. With you laying down a steady pattern of fire out here she won't suspect a thing till I grab her and take away the rifle."

"No! There's no telling what she'll do if you startle her. Go back. I'll call you when I need you."

"Verne—"

"You heard me. Get back there and help Dan keep an eye on Leroy in case he tries anything dumb."

The other muttered something unintelligible and sprinted back to his car as more shots barked from the house.

"She's got to run out of ammo sometime," Earl said.

"Around Easter, I expect. Old Clyde bought out the sporting goods when Khrushchev got in."

"Luke might be right, you know. That may be the only way to get her out of there without bloodshed."

"Forget it. The trouble with Luke Madden is he can't forget he's the one who almost got Wilbur Underhill. I'm not going to let him play hero at the expense of that frightened old woman."

"You got a better plan?"

Thickett thought. Suddenly he turned to Earl. "What's the name of that salesman from Tulsa, the one who retired and came here to live about five years ago? You know, the one Molly's sweet on?"

"Luther Briscoe?"

"Right. Ever since Clyde's death nobody's seen 'em apart, not even when she went to court. They do everything together. There's that telephone down by the highway; get hold of him and see if you can get him up here. If anybody can talk her out of there, it's Briscoe."

"I can't."

"Why not?"

"He left town yesterday to visit his sister in Kansas. He asked me to keep an eye on his house while he was gone. Said he wouldn't be back till Monday."

"Seems we can't catch a break. Well, that just leaves Plan B." Thickett jammed his pistol into his holster and unbuckled the belt.

"What are you doing?"

"I'm going in." He laid the gunbelt on the ground.

"Come again?"

"Molly and I go back. I'm counting on that to keep her from shooting me."

"*Now* who's playing hero? You can't be sure of—"

"Hold your fire, Molly!" Thickett shouted through cupped hands. "I'm coming in and I'm unarmed!"

"Don't, Vernon!" The answering bellow held a desperate edge. "I mean what I say! I'll scatter your brains all over these hills!"

"I don't think you will, Molly." Slowly he rose to his feet. A bullet spanged against the roof of the scout car.

Thickett signaled the other deputies to hold their fire and stepped clear of the car. He could see Molly's rifle pointing through the window. He took a step forward.

The second shot snatched his hat off his head. He hesitated, then moved on. A third slug whined past his ear but he kept walking. The next three shots were snapped off so rapidly they might have come from a machine gun. They struck the ground at his feet and spat gravel onto his pantlegs. By this time he was almost to the door. Two more steps and he was inside. He closed the door behind him.

It was a moment before his eyes adjusted themselves to the dim light inside the house. When they had, his first thought was that the interior hadn't changed since he was a boy. The Victorian clutter, from the overstuffed rockers shingled with doilies to the glazed china cabinets and papered walls from which hung framed and faded prints of every conceivable shape and size, was as he remembered. The only difference was the stacks and stacks of cartridge boxes on the pedestal table beside the door, and the litter of empty brass shells twinkling on the oval braided rug. Beyond it, Molly Dodd stood in the shadows at the open front window, her dark eyes glittering like the shells above the stock of the Winchester carbine she held braced against a shoulder. Thickett was looking right down its bore.

"Say your piece and get out." Her voice was taut. Small but wiry, she wore her black hair pulled straight back into a tight bun. Although her eyes were small above her hooked nose, they had a remarkable depth of expression. Her mouth was wide and turned down at the corners in a permanent scowl. Her print dress looked new, as did the sweater she wore buttoned at the neck like a cape. The firearm remained steady in her hands.

"Why don't you give me the gun, Molly?" Vernon asked quietly. "You aren't going to shoot anyone."

"When it comes to protectin' my property I'd shoot my own son if I had one," she snapped.

"You want to tell me about it?"

There was an almost indiscernible change in the expression of her eyes. "This place is mine," she said. "I know what the courts said, but they was wrong. They didn't see that record that proved Clyde paid off that loan because it don't exist no more. Not after that slippery nephew of mine got rid of it."

"Why would Leroy do that?" Thickett began to breathe a little more easily. He had her talking now.

"Why do you think? He knows there's oil on this land just like everybody else. If he can grab it for his bank he'll make himself a big man and maybe they'll forget about checkin' his books like they been threatenin' to do."

"His books?"

She nodded jerkily. Her eyes were black diamonds behind the peepsight of the rifle.

"He's been stealin' money from his accounts for years. You seen that car he drives, the clothes he wears. He can't afford them on his salary. I was in the bank once and heard a man threatenin' to take his books to the main branch in Oklahoma City and have 'em checked out. Leroy fell all over hisself tryin' to talk him out of it."

Thickett found himself growing interested in spite of the situation. "You say he destroyed the record that proved Clyde repaid the loan? Don't you have any proof of your own? What about a receipt?"

"Clyde never told me what he done with it. I been all over the house. It ain't here."

"What did you hope to gain by barricading yourself in the house?"

She smiled then, a bitter upturn of her cracked and pleated lips.

"I wanted to see that squirrel's face when I stuck this here carbine under his nose. I never meant to drag you boys into it, Vernon."

"Don't you think it's gone far enough? Come on, Molly. We're old friends. Give me the rifle."

She hesitated. Slowly the hard glitter faded from her eyes. Now she was just a tired old woman. She lowered the rifle and handed it to him.

Now that the danger was over, the deputy felt no triumph. For a long moment he regarded Molly with compassionate eyes. "What are your plans?"

"I sent my luggage on to Mexico this morning."

That was one he hadn't seen coming. "Mexico?"

"That's where Clyde and me spent our honeymoon. I got a reservation on a plane leavin' tonight from Tulsa. Don't suppose I'll make it now."

"Not if Leroy decides to press charges."

"That squirrel? Don't you worry about him. He won't do nothing that attracts attention." Her eyes strayed from his for the first time. "I sure am sorry about what I done to your car."

He laughed. "It's insured. The experience was almost worth it."

There was an embarrassed silence. Then: "What about Luther Briscoe, Molly? What was he going to think when he got back from Kansas and found you gone?"

"That's his business, I expect."

Thickett chose not to press the point. "Well," he drawled, "I'm faced with a decision. I can either put you in jail or drive you to Tulsa in time to catch your plane. Since my duty is to the citizens of Schuylerville, I think I'd be acting in their best interest if I saved them the expense of your room and board and took you to the airport."

She placed an affectionate hand on his arm. "You're a good boy, Vernon. I always said that."

It was dusk when Thickett eased the scout car he'd borrowed from Luke Madden into the parking lot in front of the sheriff's office and went in; his damaged one was in the shop. After the long drive back from Tulsa, it felt good to be using his legs again.

Earl Briggs, on his feet behind Thickett's desk, hung up the telephone as the chief deputy entered.

"I'm glad you're still here, Earl," Thickett said. "First thing tomorrow morning I want you to get in touch with the Great Midwestern Bank and Trust Company in Oklahoma City and— what is it?" The look on the boy's face sent a wave of electricity through his limbs.

Earl inclined his head toward the telephone.

"That was Leroy Cooper; in a state. He just got back to find his head cashier tied up and gagged and the rest of his employees locked in the vault. As it works out, the bank was held up for a quarter of a million dollars while we were all out at Molly's place. You'll never guess who he says did it."

Thickett felt a sinking sensation as the pieces fell into place. He tightened his grip on the doorknob. "Luther Briscoe. Molly's sweetheart."

Earl stared at him. "How on earth did you know that?"

# Flash

*When I was asked to contribute a suspense story connected with the world of sports, I thought immediately of boxing. I boxed in college; I was good, but you have to be great to keep your brains in your head where they belong. The concept of a sellout who never actually sold out spurred this one.*

Midge was glad he'd put on the electric-blue suit that day. He could use the luck.

Mr. Wassermann didn't approve of the suit. At the beginning of their professional relationship, he'd introduced Midge to his tailor, a small man in gold-rimmed glasses who looked and dressed like Mr. Wassermann, and who gently steered the big man away from the bolts of shimmering sharkskin the concern kept in stock for its gambler clients and taught him to appreciate the subtleties of gray worsted and fawn-colored flannel. He cut Midge's jackets to allow for the Glock rather than obliging him to buy them a size too large, and made his face blush when he explained the difference between "dressing left" and "dressing right." He'd never given a thought to such a thing.

The tailoring bills came out of Midge's salary, a fact for which he was more grateful than if the suits had been a gift. He was no one's charity case. The distinction was important, because he knew former fighters who stood in welfare lines and on streetcorners holding signs saying they would work for food. Back when they were at the top of the bill they had made the rounds of all the clubs with yards of gold chain around their necks, blondes on both arms, and now here they were saying they would clean out your gutters for a tuna sandwich, expecting pedestrians to feel guilty enough to buy them the sandwich and skip the gutters. Mr. Wassermann never gave anyone anything for nothing—it was a saying on the street, and Midge had heard him confirm it in person—and the big ex-fighter was proud to be able to say in return that he never took anything from anyone for nothing.

He liked the way he looked in the suits. They complemented his height without calling attention to his bulk, did not make him look poured into his clothes the way so many of his overdeveloped colleagues appeared when they dressed for the street, and if it weren't for his jagged nose and the balloons of scar tissue around his eyes he thought he might have passed for a retired NFL running back with plenty in Wall Street. Of course, that's when he wasn't walking with Mr. Wassermann, when no one would mistake him for anything but personal security.

Today, however, without giving the thing much thought, he'd decided to wear the electric-blue double-breasted he'd worn to Mr. Wassermann's office the day they'd met. He'd had on the same shade of trunks when he KO'd Lincoln Flagg at Temple Gate Arena and again when he took the decision from Sailor Burelli at Waterworks Park. He'd liked plenty of flash in those days, in and out of the ring: gold crowns, red velvet robes with Italian silk linings, crocodile luggage, yellow convertibles. Make 'em notice you, he'd thought, and you just naturally have to do your best.

But then his run had finished. He lost two key fights, his business manager decamped to Ecuador with his portfolio, the IRS attached his beach house. The last of the convertibles went back to the finance company. In a final burst of humiliation, an Internet billionaire with pimples on his forehead bought Midge's robes at auction for his weekend guests to wear around the swimming pool. When Midge had asked Mr. Wassermann for the bodyguard job, he'd been living for some time in a furnished room on Magellan Street and the electric-blue was the only suit he owned.

It had brought him luck, just as the matching trunks had. He'd gotten the job, and right away his fortunes had turned around. Because Mr. Wassermann preferred to keep his protection close, even when it was off duty, he had moved Midge into a comfortable three-room suite in the East Wing, paid for his security training, and opened an expense account for him at Rinehart's, where well-dressed salesmen advised him upon which accessories to wear with his new suits and supplied him with turtle-backed hairbrushes and the same aftershave used by the Duke of Windsor. On the rare occasions when his reclusive employer visited a restaurant (too many of his colleagues had been photographed in such establishments with their faces in their plates and bulletholes in their heads), he always asked the chef to prepare a takeout meal for Midge to eat when they returned home. These little courtesies were offered as if they were part of the terms of employment.

Because there were other bodyguards, Midge had Saturday off, and with money in the pocket of a finely tailored suit, he rarely spent them alone. The women who were drawn to the aura of sinister power that surrounded Mr. Wassermann belonged to a class Midge could not have approached when he was a mere pug. While waiting for his employer, he would see a picture of a stunning model in *Celebrity* and remember how she looked naked in his bed at the Embassy. That's when he learned about retouching.

There had been a long dry spell in that department after his last fight. True, his face had been stitched and swollen and hard to look at, but that wasn't an impediment after the Burelli decision, when eighteen inches of 4-0 thread and a patch of gauze were the only things holding his right ear to his head; he'd made the cover of *Turnbuckle* that week and signed a contract to endorse a national brand of athlete's-foot powder. He'd even considered hiring his own bodyguard to fight off the bottle-blonde waitresses. But that was when he was winning. The two big losses and particularly the stench that had clung to the twelve rounds he'd dropped to Sonny Rodriguez at the Palace Garden might as well have been a well-advertised case of the clap.

The fans had catcalled and crumpled their programs and beer cups and hurled them at the contestants. The Palace management had been forced to call the police to escort them to their dressing rooms. Three weeks later, the state boxing commission had reviewed the videotape and yanked Midge's license.

The irony was, he hadn't gone into the tank. He'd taken the money when it was offered, and since he considered himself an ethical person he'd fully intended to fake a couple of falls and force a decision against him, but he hadn't gone three rounds before he realized he was no match for the untried youngster from Nicaragua. He was out of shape and slow, and Rodriguez was graceless for all the fact that any one of his blows would have knocked down a young tree. Even the fellow who had approached Midge and ought to have known a fix from a legitimate loss called him afterward to tell him he was a rotten actor; he feared a congressional investigation.

He'd lost the fight, fair and square, so he'd felt bad about the money. He'd considered returning it, but integrity had proven to be a more complicated thing altogether than taking an honest dive. He was both a fighter who'd sold out and a fighter who'd never thrown a fight. Just trying to think where that placed him in the scheme of things made his head ache. It hurt worse than the one he'd suffered for two weeks after he went down to Ricky Shapiro.

On this particular Saturday off, he'd broken a date with a soap-opera vixen in order to meet a man with whom Mr. Wassermann sometimes did business. Angelo DeRiga—"Little Angie," Midge had heard him called, although he was not especially small, and was in fact an inch or two taller than Mr. Wassermann—dyed his hair black, even his eyebrows, and wore suits that were as well made as Midge's new ones, from material of the same good quality, but were cut too young for him. The flaring lapels and cinched waists only called attention to the fact that he was nearing sixty, just as the black hair brought out the deep lines in the artificial tan of his face. The effect was pinched and painful and increased the bodyguard's appreciation for his employer's dignified herringbones and barbered white fringe.

Little Angie shook Midge's hand at the door to his suite at the King William, complimented him upon his suit—"Flash, the genuine article," he said—and invited him to sample the gourmet spread the hotel's waiters were busy transferring from a wheeled cart to the glass-topped mahogany table in the sitting room.

Midge, who knew as well as Little Angie that the electric-blue suit was inappropriate, did not thank him, and politely refused the offer of food. He wasn't hungry, and anyway chewing interfered with his concentration. Too many blows to the head had damaged his hearing. High- and low-pitched voices were the worst, and certain labials missed him entirely. By focusing his attention on the speaker, and with the help of some amateur lip-reading, he'd managed to disguise his rather serious disability for a watchdog to have from even so observant a man as Mr. Wassermann; but then Mr. Wassermann spoke slowly, and always around the middle range. Little Angie was shrill and carried on every conversation as if he were on a fast elevator and had to finish before the car reached his floor.

When the waiters left, the two were alone with Francis, Little Angie's bodyguard. He was a former professional wrestler who shaved his head and had rehearsed his glower before a mirror until it was as nearly permanent as a tattoo. As a rule, Midge got on with other people's security, but he and Francis had disliked each other from the start. He suspected that on Francis's part this was jealousy; Mr. Wassermann's generosity to employees was well known, while Little Angie was a pinchpenny who abused his subordinates, sometimes in public. On Midge's side, he had a career prejudice against wrestlers, whom he dismissed as trained apes, and thought Francis disagreeably ugly into the bargain. When they were in the same room they spent most of the time scowling at each other. They had never exchanged so much as a word.

"I know Jake the Junkman's been white to you," Little Angie seemed to be saying; as always, Midge had to strain to make him out. "Too good, maybe. Some types need to be put on an allowance. A lot of smart guys can't handle dough."

Midge didn't like what he'd heard. Everyone knew Mr. Wassermann had made his first fortune from scrap metal, but most respected him too much to allude to his past in this offensive way. He wondered if it was his place to report the conversation to his employer. So far he didn't know why he'd been invited here.

Little Angie reached into a pocket and took out a handful of notepaper on which Midge recognized his own scrawl. "You ain't hard to track. Everywhere you go, you leave markers: Benny Royal's floating craps game on the South Side, the roulette wheel at the Kit-Kat, Gyp Handy's book up in Arbordale. There's others here. You owe twelve thousand, and you can't go to Jake for a loan. He's got a blind spot where gambling's concerned. He don't forbid his people from making a bet now and then, but he don't bail them out either. Tell me I'm wrong."

Midge shook his head. Mr. Wassermann had explained all this his first day. Midge hadn't known then that the new class of woman he'd be dating liked pretty much the same entertainments as the old.

"See, that's a problem. I spent more'n face value buying these up. I'm a reasonable man, though. I'll eat the difference. You got twelve grand, Midge?"

"You know I don't."

Little Angie smacked Midge's face with the markers.

Midge took a step forward; so did Francis. Little Angie held up a finger, stopping them both. "Let's not be uncivil. There's a way you can work it off. You won't even have to pop a sweat."

Midge heard enough of the rest to understand. Mr. Wassermann, who had the ear of a number of important people, had promised to spoil an investment Little Angie wanted to make. The important people, Little Angie hinted, would be in a position to listen to reason if Mr. Wassermann was not available to counsel them otherwise. All Midge had to do to settle his debts was stand at his usual station outside the door to Mr. Wassermann's office the following morning and not leave it, no matter what he heard going on inside.

"What if I just owe you like I did the others?" Midge asked.

"They was getting impatient. If I didn't step in, you'd be wearing plaster instead of that flashy suit, peeing through a tube. And I got to tell you, patience ain't what my what-you-call forte. Francis?"

The ugly bald wrestler produced a loop of stiff nylon fishline from a pocket. Midge knew he could prevent Francis from making use of it, but there were others in Little Angie's employ who knew what a garrote was for. He couldn't fight them all. Sooner or later he'd run into a Sonny Rodriguez.

"I know what you're thinking," Little Angie said. "There's always a place in my organization for a fellow knows the score. You won't be out of a job."

Midge hadn't been thinking about that at all. "Can I have time to think it over?"

"If I had time I'd wait for Jake to die of old age."

Midge agreed to the terms. Little Angie leered and tore up the markers. Francis looked disappointed as well as ugly.

The next morning outside Mr. Wassermann's office was as long a time as Midge had ever spent anywhere, including seven and a half rounds with Lincoln Flagg. Mr. Wassermann had some telephone calls to make and told him he'd be working through lunch, which meant Midge staying on duty, but that he'd make it up to him that night with the full twelve courses from the Bon Maison, Midge's favorite restaurant back when he was contending. He had an armchair for his personal use in the hallway, but today he couldn't stay seated in it more than three minutes at a stretch. He stood with his hands folded in front of him, then behind him, picked lint off the sleeve of his gray gabardine, found imaginary lint on the crease of the trousers and picked at that too. He was perspiring heavily under his sixty-dollar shirt, despite what Little Angie had said; he, Midge, who used to work out with the heavy bag for an hour without breaking a sweat. This selling out was hard work.

Too hard, he decided, after twenty minutes. He would take his chances with Little Angie's threats. He rapped on the door, waited the customary length of time while he assumed Mr. Wassermann was calling for him to come in, then opened the door. The garrote didn't frighten him half as much as the look of sadness he anticipated on Mr. Wassermann's face when he told him about his part in Little Angie's plan.

Mr. Wassermann was not behind his desk.

But he was.

When Midge leaned his big broken-knuckled hands on it and peered over the far edge, the first thing he saw was the tan soles of his employer's hand-lasted wingtips. Mr. Wassermann was still seated in his padded leather swivel, but the chair lay on its back. Mr. Wassermann's face was the same oxblood tint as his shoes and his tongue stuck out. Midge couldn't see the wire, but he'd heard that it sank itself so deep in a man's neck it couldn't be removed without getting blood on oneself, so most killers didn't bother to try.

A torchiere lamp behind the desk had toppled over in the struggle and lay on the carpet, its bulb shattered. Both it and Mr. Wassermann must have made more than a little noise. The door that was usually concealed in the paneling to the left stood open. It was used by Mr. Wassermann's congressmen and the occasional other business associates who preferred not to be seen going in or coming out. It was one of the worst-kept secrets around town.

Midge felt sad. He walked around the desk, stepping carefully to avoid grinding bits of glass into the Brussels carpet, and looked down into his employer's bloodshot eyes.

"The thing is, Mr. Wassermann, I didn't really go into the tank."

Mr. Wassermann didn't say anything. But then Midge probably wouldn't have heard him if he had.

# Evil Grows

*This one's about as erotic as my stuff gets. I was asked to participate in an anthology called* Flesh & Blood: Erotic Tales of Crime and Passion, *and almost begged off because I prefer subtlety to graphic sex, but when it was explained the editors were looking for something along the lines of James M. Cain's* The Postman Always Rings Twice *and* Double Indemnity—*two excellent novellas that emphasize suspense over the tiresome bedtime details—I decided to accept the challenge. Also it gave me a chance to plug a terrific pop song that never got its due.*

No, I'm not prejudiced. Well, not any more than the majority of the population. I'm an organic creature, subject to conditioning and environment, and as such I'm entitled to my own personal set of preconceptions. No, I'm not disappointed; relieved is the word. If you'd shown up with cauliflower ears or swastikas tattooed on your biceps, the interview would have been over right then. So let's sit down and jabber. What do you drink? Excuse me? Jack and *Coke*? Don't get defensive; you're young, you'll grow out of it. You grew out of your formula. Miss, my friend will have a Jack and Coke, and you can pour me another Chivas over rocks and don't let it sit too long on the bar this time. Scotch-flavored Kool-Aid is not my drink.

What's that? No, I'm not afraid she'll spit in my glass. She's got miles on her, no wedding ring, she needs this job. People will put up with what they have to, up to a point.

Which is the point where my job begins. Or began. See, I'm not sure I'm still employed. It isn't like I go to the office every day and can see if my name's still on the door. I'm talking too much; that's my third Scotch the barmaid's spitting in. You don't mind that I'm a motormouth? I forgot, you're one of the new breed. You want to know why. I'm down with that. Thank you, miss. Just keep the tab going.

Let's see. You ever watch the news, read a paper? Don't bother, that question's out of date. You can't avoid the news. The wise man on the mountain in Tibet picks up CNN in his fillings. But that's network; it's the local reports I'm talking about, the police beat. I know what you're thinking. Crime's the last thing I should be interested in when I get home. Truth is, I can't relate to wars in eastern Europe, not since I got too old for the draft, but give me a carjacking two streets over from where I live and you can't pry me away from the screen. Past forty you get selective about what you take in. I'm not just talking about your stomach.

Anyway, have you noticed, once or twice a month there's a story about some schnook getting busted trying to hire a hit man? Some woman meets a guy in a bar and offers him like a thousand bucks to knock off her husband or boyfriend or her husband's girlfriend or the mother of the girl who's beating out her daughter for captain of the cheerleading squad? Okay, it's not always a woman, but let's face it, they're still the designated child-bearers, it's unnatural for them to take life. So they engage a surrogate. The reason they get caught is the surrogate turns out to be an undercover cop. I mean, it happens so often you wonder if there aren't more cops out there posing as hit men than there are hit men. Which may be true, I don't know. Assassins don't answer the census.

That's how it seems, and the department's just as happy to let people think that. Actually there's very little happenstance involved. The woman's so pissed she tells her plans to everyone she knows and a few she doesn't, gets a couple of margaritas in her and tells the bartender. Working up her courage, see, or maybe just talking about it makes her feel better, as if she went ahead and did it. So in a week or so twenty people are in on the secret. Odds are pretty good one of them's a cop. I don't know a bookie who'd bet against at least one of them *telling* a cop. So the next Saturday night she's sitting in a booth getting blasted and a character in a Harley jacket with Pennzoil in his hair slides in, buys her a zombie and a beer for himself, and says I understand you're looking for someone to take care of a little problem. Hey, nothing's subtle in a bar. People want their mechanics to be German and their decorators gay, and when they decide to have someone iced they aren't going to hire someone who looks like Hugh Grant.

You'll be happy to hear, if you're concerned about where civilization is headed, that many of these women, once they realize what's going on, are horrified. Or better yet, they laugh in the guy's face. These are the ones that are just acting out. The only blood they intend to draw will be in the courtroom, if it ever gets that far; a lot of couples who considered murder go on to celebrate their golden anniversaries. A good cop, or I should say a good person who is a cop, will draw away when he realizes it's a dry hole. It's entrapment if he pushes it, and anyway what's the point of removing someone from society who wasn't a threat to begin with? It just takes time away from investigations that might do some good. Plus he knows the next woman he invites himself to will probably take him up on it.

Hell yes, he's wearing a wire, and I'm here to tell you Sir Laurence Olivier's got nothing on an undercover stiff who manages to appear natural knowing he can't squirm around or even lift his glass at the wrong time because the rustle of his clothing might drown out the one response he needs to make his case. I was kidding about the Harley jacket; leather creaks like a bitch, on tape it sounds like a stand of giant sequoias making love, and you don't want to hear about corduroy or too much starch in a cotton shirt. Even when you wear what's right and take care, you need to find a way to ask the same question two or three times and get the same answer, just for insurance. Try and pull that off without tipping your mitt. I mean, everyone's seen *NYPD Blue*. So you begin to see, as often as these arrests make news, the opportunity comes up oftener yet. You can blame Hollywood if you like, or maybe violent video games. I'm old enough to remember when it was comic books. My old man had a minister when he was ten who preached that Satan spoke through *Gang Busters* on the radio. My opinion? We've been killers since the grave.

Lest you think I draw my munificent paycheck hanging around gin mills hitting on Lizzie Borden, I should tell you life undercover most of the time is about as exciting as watching your car rust. When the lieutenant told me to meet this Rockover woman I'd been six weeks raking leaves in the front yard of a drug lord in Roseville, posing as a gardener. I never saw the man; he's in his bedroom the whole time, flushing out his kidneys and playing euchre. He's got maybe a year to live, so assuming I do gather enough for an indictment, he'll be in hell trumping Tupac's hand by the time they seat the jury. I don't complain when I'm pulled off. Friend, I'd work Stationary Traffic, handing out parking tickets, if it meant getting out of those goddamn overalls.

The briefing's a no-brainer. This Nola Rockover has had it with her boss. He's a lawyer and a sexual harasser besides, it's a wonder the Democrats haven't tapped him for the nomination. It's her word against his, and he's a partner in the firm, so you know who's going to come out on the short end if she reports him. Her career's involved. Admit it, you'd take a crack at him yourself. That's how you know it's worth investigating. The odd thing, one of the odd things about getting a conviction, is the motive has to make sense. Some part of you has to agree with the defendant in order to hang him. It's a funny system.

Getting ready for a sting you've got to fight being your own worst enemy. You can't ham it up. I've seen cops punk their hair and pierce their noses—Christ, their tongues and bellybuttons too—and get themselves tossed by a nervous bouncer before they even make contact, which is okay because nine times out of ten the suspect will take one look at them and run for the exit. I know what I said about bars and subtlety, but they're no place for a cartoon either. So what I do is leave my hair shaggy from the gardening job, pile on a little too much mousse, go without shaving one day, put on clean chinos and combat boots and a Dead T-shirt—a little humor there, it puts people at ease—and mostly for my own benefit I clip a teeny gold ring onto my left earlobe. You have to look close to see it doesn't go all the way through. I've spent every day since the academy trying to keep holes out of me and I'm not about to give up for one case. Now I look like an almost-over-the-hill Deadhead who likes to hip it up on weekends; a turtleneck and a sportcoat on Casual Friday is as daring as he gets during the week. Point is not so much to look like a hit man as to not look like someone who isn't. Approachability's important.

The tech guy shaves a little path from my belt to my solar plexus, tapes the mike and wire flat, the transmitter to my back just above the butt-crack. The T's loose and made of soft cotton, washed plenty of times. Only competition I have to worry about is the bar noise. Fortunately, the Rockover woman's Saturday night hangout is a family-type place: you know, where a kid can drink a Coke and munch chips from a little bag while his parents visit with friends over highballs. Loud drunks are rare, there's a juke but no band. The finger's a co-worker in the legal firm. I meet him at the bar, he points her out, I thank him and tell him to blow. First I have to reassure him I'm not going to throw her on the floor and kneel on her back and cuff her like on *Cops*; he's more worried she'll get herself in too deep than about what she might do to the boss. I go along with this bullshit and he leaves. Chances are he's got his eye on her job, but he hasn't got the spine not to feel guilty about it.

The place is crowded and getting noisy, the customers are starting to unwind. I order a Scotch and soda, heavy on the fizz, wait for a stool, and watch her for a while in the mirror. She's sitting at the bar booth facing another woman near the shuffleboard table, smoking a cigarette as long as a Bic pen and nursing a clear drink in a tall glass, vodka and tonic probably. I'm hoping I'll catch her alone sometime during the evening, maybe when the friend goes to the can, which means I don't count on getting any evidence on tape until I convince her to ditch the friend. So I wait and watch.

Which in this case is not unpleasant.

Nola Rockover's a fox. Not, I hasten to add, one of those pneumatically enhanced bimbos you see on TV, just another flavor-of-the-month, but the dark, smoldering kind you hardly ever see except in black-and-white movies and old reruns. She's a brunette, slender—not thin, I've had it with those anorexic bonepiles that make you want to abduct them and tie them down and force-feed them mashed potatoes until they at least cast a decent shadow—I'm talking lithe and sinuous, like a dancer, with big dark eyes and prominent cheekbones. She had a pantherish quality I'd come to know better, and how.

She wore this dark sleeveless top and some kind of skirt, no cleavage or jewelry except for a thin gold necklace that called attention to the long smooth line of her throat, and she had a way of holding her chin high, almost aloof but not quite, more like she hadn't forgotten what her mother had told her about the importance of good posture. She's not talking, except maybe to respond to something the other woman is saying, encourage her to go on, except I'm thinking she's not really that interested, just being polite. In any case it's her friend who's flapping her chin and waving her hands around like she's swatting hornets. Probably describing her love life.

Yes, miss, another Chivas, and how's yours? Sure? Now you're making me look like a lush.

Nola's friend? Okay, so I'm a chauvinist pig. Maybe she's talking about the Red Wings. She's got on this ugly business suit with a floppy bow tie, like she hasn't been to see a movie since *Working Girl*. I'm thinking Nola tolerates her company to avoid drinking alone in public. Maybe she already suspects she's said too much in that condition in the past. You can see I'm kindly disposed to her before I even make contact. There's no rule says you can't like 'em and cuff 'em.

I watch twenty minutes, my drink's all melted ice, and I'm starting to think this other woman's got a bladder the size of Toledo when she finally gets up and goes to wee-wee. I give it a minute so as not to look like a shark swimming in, then I wander on over. Nola's getting out another cigarette and I'm wishing, not for the first time, I hadn't given up the weed, or I could offer to light her up from the Zippo I no longer carried. Sure, it's corny, but it works. That's how some things stay around long enough to get corny. But it's out, so I do the next best thing and say, "I hear the surgeon general frowns on those."

She looks up slowly like she knows I've been standing there the whole time, and you'll like what she says.

"I don't follow generals' orders any more. I got my discharge."

And she smiles, this cool impersonal number that make the soles of my feet tingle. She's got nice teeth—not perfect, one incisor's slightly crooked, but she keeps them white, which is not easy when you smoke. Her eyes don't smile, though. Even if I didn't know her recent history I'd guess this was someone for whom life has not come with greased wheels.

I'm scraping my skull for what to say next when she throws me a life preserver. "You like the Dead?"

Now, that's a conversation starter. It takes me a second to remember what's on my T-shirt.

Not, "You're a Deadhead?" Which is a term they know in Bowling Green by now, it's hip no more, but most people are afraid not to use it for fear of appearing unhip. The way she doesn't say it, though, tells me she's so hip she doesn't even bother to think about it. I admit that's a lot to get out of four words, but that was Nola, a living tip-of-the-iceberg. Thanks, honey; I like my Scotch good and orange.

I lost the thread. Oh, right, the Dead. I take a chance. Remember, everything hangs on how I broach the subject, and the conventional wisdom is never, ever jump the gun. If opening it up standing in front of her table with her friend about to come back from the can any second is not jumping it, I don't know what is.

"Yeah, I like the dead."

Lowercase, no cap. Which you may argue makes no difference when you're talking, but if you do, good day to you, because you're not the person for what I have in mind. No comment? There's hope for you. Then you'll appreciate her reaction.

Her face went blank. No expression, it might have been enameled metal with the eyes painted on. She'd heard that small *d*, caught on right away, and quick as a switch she'd shut down the system. She wasn't giving me anything. Wherever this went, it was up to me to take it from there.

"I know about your problem," I said. "I can help."

She didn't say, "What problem?" That would have disappointed me. Her eyes flick past my shoulder, and I know without looking her friend's coming. "Have you got a card?"

This time I smile. "You mean like 'Have gun, will travel'?"

She doesn't smile back. "I'm known here. I'll be at the Hangar in an hour." And then she turns her head and I'm not there.

I join the boys in the van, who take off their earphones long enough to agree the Hangar is Smilin' Jack's Hangar, a roadhouse up in Oakland County that's been around since there was a comic-strip character of that name, a trendy spot once that now survives as a place where the laws of marriage don't apply. Every community needs a place to mess around.

So forty minutes later wearing fresh batteries I'm groping through the whiskey-sodden dark of a building that was once an actual hangar for a small air service, my feet not touching the floor because the bass is so deep from the juke it suspends everything on vibration alone. When I find a booth not currently being used for foreplay and order the house Scotch, I'm hoping Nola is part bat, because the teeny electric lamp on the table is no beacon.

At the end of ten minutes, right on time, I catch a whiff of scent and then she rustles into the facing seat. She's freshened her make-up, and with that long dark hair in an underflip and the light coming up from below leaving all the shadows where they belong, she looks like someone I wish I had a wife to cheat on with. The perfume is some kind of moon-flowering blossom, dusky. Don't look for it, it wouldn't smell the same on anyone else.

"Who are you?" She doesn't even wait for drinks.

"Call me Ted."

"No good. If you know my situation you know both my names."

I grin. "Ted Hazlett." Which is a name I use sometimes. It's close to "hazard," but not so close they won't buy it.

"And what do you do, Ted Hazlett?"

"This and that."

"Where do you live?"

"Here and there. We can do this all night if you like."

My Scotch comes by slow freight. She orders vodka tonic, and when the waiter's gone she settles back and lights up one of those long cigarettes.

"We're just two people talking," she says. "No law against that."

"Not according to the ACLU."

"'This and that.' Which one is you kill people?"

I think this over carefully. "'That.'"

She nods, like it's the right answer.

She tells her story then, and there's nothing incriminating in the way she tells it, at least not against her. She's a paralegal with a downtown firm whose name I know, having been cross-examined by some of its personnel in the past. Attends law school nights, plans someday to practice family law, except this walking set of genitalia she's assigned to, partner in the firm, is planning even harder to get into her pants.

You know the drill: whispered obscenities in her ear when they're alone in the office, anonymous gifts of crotchless panties and front-loading bras mailed to her apartment, midnight phone calls when she's too groggy to cut him off in the middle of the first heavy breath. At first she's too scared to file a complaint, knowing there's no evidence that can be traced to him. Then comes the day he tells her she better go down on him if she wants a job evaluation that won't get her fired.

The firm's as old as habeas; no employee recommendation means no employment with any other firm. To top it off, this scrotum, this partner, sits on the board of the school she attends and is in a position to expel her and wipe out three years of credits. Any way you look at it he's got her by the smalls.

Well, what's a girl to do? She's no Shirley Temple; lived with a guy for two years, object matrimony, until she caught him in the shower with a neighbor and threw his clothes out a window—I mean every stitch, he had to go out in a towel to fetch them. The senior partners are conservative about cohabitation outside marriage and domestic disturbance.

So she does the deed on the partner, thinking to hand in her two weeks' notice the next day and take her good references to a firm where oral examinations are not required.

Except she's so good at it the slob threatens to withhold references if she refuses to assign herself to him permanently, so to speak.

After stewing it over, she decides to take it up with the head of the outfit, file a complaint. But the senior to the seniors won't sully himself, and fobs her off on an assistant, who by the time she finishes her story has pegged her as an immoral bitch who's gone to blackmail when she found out she couldn't advance herself on her knees; she can see it in his face when he tells her the incident will be taken into advisement.

Next day she's reassigned to computer filing; the dead end of dead ends and leverage to hound her into resigning.

It doesn't stop there. She tries to finance a new car but her credit's bad. Pulls out her card to buy a blouse at Hudson's, the clerk makes a call, then cuts up the card in front of her. Some more shit like that happens, then late one night she gets another phone call. It's the walking genitalia, telling her he's got friends all over and if she isn't nice to him he'll phony up her employment record, get her fired, evict her, frame her for soliciting, whatever; it's him or a cell at County, followed by accommodations in a refrigerator carton on Woodward Avenue; choice is yours, baby. He's psycho, no question, but he's a psycho with connections.

What the partner hasn't figured on is a basic law of nature: Corner an animal, and it's got only one way out.

There's no way I can tell you all this the way Nola told it. She lays it out flat, just the facts, without a choke or a sob. The only hint she's stinging at all is when she breaks a sentence in half to sip her drink, like a runner taking a hint of oxygen before he can go on. But I know every word's true. I can see this puffed-up bastard in his Armani, ripping up some poor schmoe in court for stepping out on his wife, then rushing back to the office for his daily hummer from the good-looking paralegal. And while I'm seeing this—I can't say even now if I knew I was aware of it—I sneak a hand up under my shirt and disconnect the wire.

Nola won't talk business in a bar. She suggests we meet at her place the next night and gives me an address on East Jefferson. I stand up when she does, pay for the drinks—there's no discussion on that, it's an assumption we both make—and I go to the can, mainly to give her a chance to make some distance before I meet with the crew in the van. Only when I leave the roadhouse, I know she's somewhere out there in the dark, watching me.

I walk right past the van and get into my car and pull out. I don't even give the earlobe-tug that tells them I'm being watched, because I *know* Nola would recognize it for what it was. And I spent an extra fifteen minutes crazying up the way home, just in case she's following me. You know, they say some prey has a way of turning things around on the hunter; that's Nola Rockover in a nutshell.

My telephone's ringing when I get in, and I'm not surprised it's Carpenter, from the van.

"What's the deal, something go wrong with the transmitter, you forgot we're out there freezing our nuts off? You get drunk or what?"

"Sorry, I'm wiped out. Wire must've come loose. Not to worry, Phil. She's no killer, just a broad looking for a sympathetic ear. She couldn't kill her drink, much less her piece-of-shit boss."

"So why give us the brush off?"

But I was ready for that, too. "Bartender was giving me the fisheye. He saw me climbing in and out of a van I might blow his Tuesday night poker game in the back room. We need places like that, if just for seed."

I don't know if he believed me about Nola, but the part about the bartender was true enough based on what we knew about the dive, so he let it go. Carpenter's not what you call Supercop, would just as soon duck the graveyard shift for whatever reason. It wasn't for fear of his disapproval I stayed awake most of that night wishing I still smoked. I could still smell her cigarettes and that dusky scent on my clothes.

Most of the next day was paperwork pertaining to the nonexistent Rockover case. I logged out in time to go home and freshen up and put on a sport shirt and slacks, no sense working on the image now that the hook's in.

Understand, I had no intention of whacking the son of a bitch who was bringing her grief. In twelve years with the department I'd never even fired my piece except to qualify. I'm sympathetic to her case, maybe I can help her figure a way out—brace the creep and apply a little strong-arm if necessary, see will he pick on someone his own size and gender.

Okay, and maybe wrangle myself some pussy while I'm at it. Hey, we're both single, and it's been a stretch for me, what with everyone so scared of AIDS and GHB; I'm telling you, the alphabet's played hell with the mating game. I figure I'm still leagues above the prick in the thousand-dollar suit.

She's on the second floor of one of those converted warehouses in what is now called Rivertown, with a view of the water through a plate-glass window the size of a garage door in her living room. Décor's sleek, all chrome and glass and black leather and a spatter of paint in a steel frame on one wall, an Impressionist piece that when you stand back turns out to be of a nude woman reclining, who looks just enough like Nola I'm afraid to ask if she posed for it. I can tell it's good, but the colors are all wrong: bilious green and violent purple and a kind of rusty brown that I can only describe as dried blood, not a natural flesh tone in the batch. It puts me in mind less of a beautiful naked woman than a jungle snake coiled around a tree limb. Artists, they see things most of the rest of us miss.

It takes me a while to take all this in, because it's Nola who opens the door for me. She's wearing a dark turtleneck top over skin-tight stirrup pants with the straps under her bare feet, which are long and narrow, with high arches and clear polish on the toenails. Those perfect feet are just about the only skin she's showing, but I'm telling you, I was glad I brought a bottle of wine to hold in front of myself. It's like high school, with the hormones kicking in.

She takes the bottle with thanks, her eyes flicker down for a split second, and the corners of her lips turn up the barest bit, but she says nothing. I step inside and she closes the door, locking it with a crisp little snick.

Charlie Parker's playing low on a sound system I never did get to see. She has me open the wine using a wicked-looking corkscrew in the tiny kitchen, and we go to the living room and drink from stemware and munch on crackers she's set out on a tray on the glass coffee table, crumbly things that dissolve into butter on the tongue. I'm sitting on the black sofa, legs crossed, her beside me with her legs curled under her, as supple as the snake-woman in the picture, giving off that scent.

Small talk, music, wine. Then she lifts her glass to her lips and asks me if I approve of the police department's retirement package.

I managed not to choke on my wine. I uncross my legs, lean forward, set my glass on the table, sit back. I could try to bluff it out, but just from my exposure to her I know it'd be a waste of breath. I asked her how she doped it out.

"You forget I'm a file clerk now. I ran that name you gave me through the computer. You shouldn't have used one you'd used before. Are you getting all this on tape?"

"I'm not wearing a wire."

"Am I supposed to believe that?"

"Oh, I was wearing one before, but I yanked it. I want to help."

She watches me, unblinking as a snake.

"Lady," I said, "if it's a lie, you'd be in custody right now."

She watches me a beat more, then sets down her glass, and before I know it she's unbuttoning my shirt.

Long after it's obvious there's nothing under it but me, she goes on groping; and in a little while I know there's nothing but Nola under the sweater and pants. It's like wrestling that snake, only a warm-blooded one with a quicker tongue that tastes like wine when it's in my mouth and burns like fire when it's working its way down my chest, and down and down while I'm digging holes in the leather upholstery with my fingers, trying to hang on.

I don't want to give you the impression I'm one of those jerks that tries to puff himself up by giving the play-by-play; I just want you to see how a fairly good cop brain melted down before Nola's heat. I've been married, and I've had my hot-and-heavies, but I've never even *read* about some of the things we did that night. We're on the sofa, we're off the sofa, the table tips over and we're heaving away in spilled wine and bits of broken crystal; I can show you a hundred healed-over cuts on my back even now and you'd think I got tangled in barbed wire. In a little while we're both slick with wine and sweat and various other bodily fluids, panting like a pair of wolves, and we're still going at it. I'm not sure they'd chance showing it on the Playboy Channel.

Miss? Oh, miss? Ice water, please. I'm burning up.

That's better. Whew! When I think about that night—hell, whenever I think about Nola—this song keeps running through my head. It isn't what Bird Parker was playing on the CD, he died years before it came out. It wasn't a hit, although it should have been, it was haunting. I don't even know who recorded it. "Evil Grows," I think it was called, and it was all about this poor schnook realizing his girl's evil and how every time he looks at her, evil grows in him. Whoever wrote it might have known Nola. Because by the time I crawled out of that apartment just before dawn, feeling like I'd been through a grain combine, I'd made up my mind to kill her boss for her.

His name's Ethan Hollis, and he's living beyond his means in Grosse Pointe, but if they outlaw that they'll have to throw a prison wall around that place. I don't need to park more than two minutes in front of the big Georgian he shares with his wife to know it won't happen in there, inside a spiked fence with the name of his alarm company on a tin sign on the gate.

Anyway, since I'm not the only one who's heard Nola's threats, we've agreed that apparent accidental death is best; I'm just taking stock. The few seconds I get to see him through binoculars, coming out on the porch to tell the gardener he isn't clipping the hedge with his little finger extended properly—is enough to make me hate him, having worked that very job under cover for a drug lord in Roseville. He's chubbier than I had pictured, a regular teddy bear with curly dark hair on his head and a Rolex on his fat wrist, with a polo shirt, yet. He deserves to die for no other reason than his lack of fashion sense.

I know his routine thanks to Nola, but I follow him for a week, just to look. I've taken personal time, of which I've built up about a year. The guy logs four hours total in the office. The rest of the time he's lunching with clients, golfing with the senior partner, putting on deck shoes and dorky white shorts and pushing a speedboat up and down the river, that sort of bullshit. Drowning would be nice, except I'd join him, because I can't swim and am no good on the water.

These are my days. Nights I'm with Nola, working our way through the *Kama Sutra* and adding footnotes of our own.

The only time I can expect Hollis to be alone without a boat involved is when he takes his Jaguar for a spin. It's his toy, he doesn't share it. Trouble is not even Nola knows when he'll get the urge. So every day when he's home I park around the corner and trot back to his north fence, watching for that green convertible. It's a blind spot to the neighbors, too, and for the benefit of passersby I'm wearing a jogging suit; just another fatcat following the surgeon general's advice.

Four days in, nothing comes through that gate but Hollis's black Mercedes, either with his wife on the passenger's side or just him taking a crowded route through heavy traffic to work or the country club.

I'm losing confidence. I figure I can get away with the jogging gag maybe another half a day before someone gets nervous and calls the cops. I'm racking my brain for some other cover when out comes the Jag, spitting chunks of limestone off the inside curves of the driveway. I hustle back to my car.

Hollis must need unwinding, because he's ten miles over the limit and almost out of sight when I turn out of the side street.

North is the choice today. In a little while we're up past the lake, with the subdivisions thinning out along a two-lane blacktop. It's a workday—Nola's in the office, good alibi—and for miles we're almost the only two cars, so I'm hanging back, but I can tell he's not paying attention to his rearview or he'd open it up and leave me in the dust. The arrogant son of a bitch thought he was invulnerable.

You see how I'm taking every opportunity to work up a good hate? I've had time to lose my sense of commitment, start to think when I get him alone I'll work him over, whisper in his ear what's in store if he doesn't lay off diddling the help. He's such a soft-looking slob I know he'll cave in if I just knock out a tooth.

After ninety minutes we've left the blacktop and are towing twin streamers of dust down a dirt road with farms on both sides and here and there a copse of trees left for windbreaks. Now it's time to open the ball.

I've got police lights installed inside the radiator grille, and as I press down the accelerator I flip them on. Now he finds his mirror, gooses the pedal, then thinks better of it and begins to slow down. But we're short of the next copse of trees, so I close in and encourage him forward, then as we enter the shade I signal him to pull over.

I've been wearing my old uniform under the jogging suit all this time, and have shucked off the outer shell while driving. I put on my cap and get out and approach the Jag with my hand resting on my sidearm. The driver's window purrs down, he flashes his pearlies nervously. "Was I speeding, Officer?"

"Step out of the car, please."

He's got his wallet out. "I have my license and registration."

I tell him again to step out of the car.

He looks surprised, but he puts the wallet away and grasps the door handle. His jaw's set. I can see he thinks it's a case of mistaken identity and he may have a lucrative harassment suit if he can make himself disagreeable enough. I've been around enough lawyers to know how they think; meth cookers are better company.

Then his face changes again. He's staring at the uniform.

"You're pretty far out of your jurisdiction, aren't you? This area is patrolled by the county sheriff."

"Get out of the fucking car." I draw my sidearm.

"Fuck you, fake cop." He floors it.

But it's a gravel road, and the tires spin for a second, spraying pebbles, which strike my legs and sting like hornets, which gives me the mad to make that lunge and grab the window post with my free hand. Just then the tread bites and the Jag spurs ahead and I know I'm going to be dragged if I don't let go or stop him.

I don't let go. I stick the muzzle of my piece through the window, cocking the hammer.

Who knows but it might have worked, if my fingers didn't slip off the window post. As I fall away from the car I strike my other wrist against the post and a round punches a hole through the windshield.

Hollis screams. He thinks he's hit, takes his hands off the wheel, and that's the last I see of him until after the Jag plunges into a tree by the side of the road. The bang's so loud if you even heard my piece go off you'd forget about it because the second report sounds like a cannon, and across a whole field of wheat at that.

I get up off the ground and spring to the car, still holding the gun. The hood's folded like a road map, the radiator pouring steam, windshield gone. I look up and down the road and across the field opposite the stand of trees. Not a soul in sight, if you don't count a cow looking our way.

Just as I'm starting to appreciate my lucky break, I hear moaning. Lawyers are notoriously hard to kill.

He lifts his head from the wheel. The forehead's split, the face a sheet of blood. It looks bad enough to finish him even if it wasn't instantaneous, but I'm no doctor.

I guess you could say I panicked. I reached through the window and hit him with the butt of the gun, how many times I don't know, six or seven or maybe a dozen. The bone of his forehead started to make squishing sounds like ice cracking under your feet, squirting water up through the fissures. Only in this case it wasn't water, and I know I'm going to have to burn the uniform because my gun arm is soaked to the elbow with blood and gray ooze. Finally I stop swinging the gun and feel for a pulse in his carotid.

He wasn't using it any more. I holstered the weapon, took his head in both hands, and rested his squishy brow against the steering wheel where it had struck the first time.

I take a last look around to make sure I didn't drop anything, get into my car, and leave, making sure first to drag the jogging suit back on over my gory uniform. I wink at the cow on my way past.

For the next few days I stay clear of Nola. I don't even call, knowing she'll hear about it on the news; I can't afford anyone seeing us together. I guess I was being overcautious. Hollis's death was investigated as an accident, and at the end of a week the sheriff tells the press the driver lost control on loose gravel. I guess the cow didn't want to get involved.

I was feeling good about myself. I didn't see any need to wrestle with my conscience over the death of a sexual predator, and a high-price lawyer to boot. As is the way of human nature I patted my own back for a set of fortunate circumstances I'd had no control over. I was starting to think God was on my side.

But Nola isn't.

When I finally visited, after the cops had paid their routine call and gone away satisfied her beef with her employer was unconnected with an accident upstate, she gave me hell for staying away, accused me of cowardly leaving her to face the police alone. I settled her down finally, but I could see my explanation didn't satisfy. As I'm taking off my coat to get comfortable she tells me she has an early morning, everyone at the office is working harder in Hollis's absence and she needs her sleep. This is crap, because Hollis was absent almost as often when he was alive, but I leave.

She doesn't answer her phone for two days after that. When I go to the apartment her bell doesn't answer and her car isn't in the port. I come back another night, same thing. I lean against the building groping in my pockets, forgetting I don't smoke anymore, then Nola's old yellow Camaro swings in off Jefferson and I step back into the shadows, because there are two people in the front seat. I watch as the lights go off and they get out.

"If you're that afraid of him, why don't you call the police?" A young male voice, belonging to a slender figure in a green tank top and torn jeans.

"Because he *is* the police. Oh, Chris, I'm terrified. He won't stop hounding me this side of the grave." And saying this Nola huddles next to him and hands him her keys to open the front door, which he does one-handed, his other arm being curled around her waist.

They go inside, and the latch clicking behind them sounds like the coffin lid shutting in my face. She's got a new shark in her school. I'm the chum she's feeding him. And I know without having to think about it that I've killed this schnook Ethan Hollis for the same reason Chris is going to kill me; I've run out of uses. So for Chris, now *I'm* the sexual predator.

Until I got a good look at her in the security light, I wasn't sure it was even her. She hadn't pulled that helpless-female routine with me. To hear her now, she hadn't a sardonic bone in her body. See, I'd been wrong to connect her with just one variety of reptile. She's at least half chameleon, changing her colors to suit the sap of the moment.

I was out of my league.

That's why we're talking now. It's Nola or me, and I need to be somewhere else when she has her accident. I've got a feeling I'm not in the clear over Hollis. Call it cop's intuition, but I've been part of the community so long I know when I've been excluded. Even Phil Carpenter won't look me in the eye when we're talking about the Pistons. I've been tagged.

Except you're not going to kill Nola, sweetie. No, not because you're a woman; you girls have moved into every other profession, why not this? You're not going to do it because you're a cop.

Forget how I know. Say a shitter knows a shitter and leave it there. What? Sure, I noticed when you reached up under your blouse. I thought at the time you were adjusting your bra, but— well, that was before I said I'd decided to kill Hollis, wasn't it? I hope your crew buys it, two wires coming loose in the same cop's presence within a couple of weeks. I'll leave first so you can go out to the van and tell them the bad news. I live over on Howard. Well, you know the address. You bring the wine—no Jack and Coke, mind—I'll cook the steaks. I think I can finish convincing you about Nola.

Like killing a snake.

# The Bog

*I hesitated over this one for reasons similar to those of my unnamed narrator, to sacrifice a good story idea in order to commit the perfect murder. In my case, I had to let go of the perfect murder in order to write a story. (Confess: You've fantasized along these lines yourself.) But then I probably wouldn't kill anyone anyway, and there's no sense letting a good idea go begging.*

Watching Hufnagel take the strychnine, I felt a twinge of remorse.

Certainly not for Hufnagel, or for the fact that the *primo* cocaine he thought he was ingesting contained enough mole poison to ensure the pristine character of every lawn in suburban Michigan. He'd bought that fate five years before, when he plagiarized one of my best ideas and pissed it away on a desk-top novel that languished in Barnes & Noble and died on the remaindering table, forever beyond the reach of a writer who knew best how to make use of the subject matter. I'd have taken him out then, but there'd have been scant satisfaction in an act performed in the heat of first wrath. The thing needed time; to plan, to refine, to make friendly overtures, to overcome through patience and grim sincerity the natural suspicions of a thief whose victim has elected not only to forgive him, but to include him in his circle of intimates. The *center* of the circle.

The best con men, they say, con themselves first. It was necessary to remind myself of how close we were before the betrayal, in effect to erase all surface memory of the incident and re-create emotions formed in an innocence I no longer possessed. Fortunately, good writers and method actors have that ability in common, and if I may say so I succeeded as thoroughly as an Olivier, a James Dean. There had even been times, dining and drinking with the man I despised above all others, when I felt as close to him as a brother, and when thoughts of the despicable theft occurred unbidden, managed without much effort to convince myself it had all been a mistake, a laughable coincidence, and that since he'd failed so miserably to profit from it, that the thing was of no great consequence.

But an actor or a writer who is unable to separate himself from his self-delusion when not actually performing is a tiresome creature. A good con man never loses sight of the prize. In my mind, Hufnagel was as dead as the idea he'd appropriated and defiled with his hackery. It was a corpse I sat beside at ballgames. It was a cadaver I invited to my home in the country. All that remained was to put the concept into practice.

No, it wasn't Hufnagel who made me contrite, and I'd lived with the plan too long to feel guilty for my deception. I grieved for the loss of another idea. It was as good as or better than one he'd stolen, there was an Edgar Award in it at least if I used it in fiction, and once I'd used it in fact, it would be lost to me forever. While writers make their best work public, murderers bury theirs. It's a near thing for an artist or an entertainer to seek success through obscurity.

But a twinge was all it was. Ideas aren't hard to come by, unless you're so deficient creatively to have to filch them. I didn't lament the one he'd made away with so much as the making away. The hard part had been winning his trust, and convincing him that I shared his drug habit. I drink in moderation, smoke not at all, and had been pompous on the point that I'd never taken an illegal substance. So in order to get the strychnine into my enemy, I was forced to present myself as a liar and a hypocrite. It was humiliating, especially considering the audience, to suffer his blubbery, condescending grin when at last he'd accepted my admission. *So you're no better than me after all*, it said, complete with his indifference to elementary grammar.

No matter. It was a corpse's grin.

I'm nothing if not a thorough researcher. I had no trouble getting him to believe that the Ziploc bag I showed him contained the purest cocaine from the coastal village of Canavieiras, at a cost commensurate with its quality.

He actually licked his lips when he saw the flaky white powder. "Your books must be in the black finally."

"When did poverty ever stop one of us?" I placed a shaving mirror on the coffee table, picked up a razor blade, and separated the little heap I'd poured on the glass into parallel lines, as neatly as if I'd been practicing for years instead of hours.

I wasn't a good host. I helped myself first, to remove any lingering doubt on his part. It was unnecessary. He was so intent on his own approaching pleasure he didn't notice that what I inhaled through the rolled-up dollar bill was empty air from an unoccupied part of the mirror. Impatient as he was, he didn't bother to count the remaining lines. I'd expected that. There's no underestimating the greed of a plagiarist, especially one who is also a drug fiend. He seized the bill, bent to the line nearest him where he sat on the sofa, and made an appropriately porcine noise snorting it up into his nasal cavity, into his empty brain.

Would he have time to notice it was only all-purpose flour, or would the sting of the poison convince him it was as advertised? Even cyanide doesn't work as swiftly as you'd think on the evidence of what some of my mystery-writing colleagues publish. But when you hate a man, truly detest him enough to see him punished, strychnine's the thing. While it takes ten or twenty minutes for symptoms to appear when ingested internally (much less when taken directly into the exposed capillaries inside the nose), the time spent in violent convulsion is an eternity for the victim. Puzzling visibly over the immediate sensation, given the build-up I'd provided, he reached back a hand to massage his stiff neck. When he moved it around to probe at his face, stiffening as well, I got up from the sofa. I did this as much to remove myself from the range of his flailing arms and legs as to watch the show.

It was a hit. He crashed to the floor, knocking over the table and scattering its contents, rolled onto his back, and arched his stomach toward the ceiling, keeping his head and feet on the floor. (One of the accepted positions for both Lamaze and death throes.) His entire body quivered like a drawn bow. Spittle formed at the corners of his mouth, which drew farther and farther apart in a rictus that was not at all similar to the superior leer he'd worn only minutes before. His face looked slimy. He sweated through his sports shirt, he made a gurgling noise in his throat that may have been an attempt to cry for help. He released the contents of his bladder.

Enough detail. I'm not a sadist. Soon enough he was dead, and I got to work.

The beauty part of the plan wasn't the murder; that was pedestrian. It was the disposal of the body. That's where most amateurs foul up, for not thinking things through. Either they chopped up the remains and parted them out, multiplying the chances of discovery, or buried them in a flowerbed or something on their own property or—just as bad—tossed them in the trunk of a car and drove to some secluded spot, risking a police pullover for a cracked taillight or failure to sign a turn or just because the cop was bored and wanted someone to talk to, and even if they succeeded and got back home undetected and removed all traces of the body from the trunk, some crime-lab geek going over the corpse collected traces of the trunk from the body, which was a guaranteed conviction. You couldn't count on the remains not being found, not completely, and you had to prepare for the possibility that you'd be suspected and questioned.

With the advance from a three-book contract, I'd bought a house on a hundred acres in the country. It was mostly wilderness: hills good for hiking and not much else, patches of woods and swamp. A lot of empty acreage, perfect for keeping the neighbors at arm's length and a writer in solitude. At the back, it bordered on a farm belonging to an old recluse named Lundergaard, whose wife had left him forty years ago, after which he'd retired from the world, working his field for his own subsistence and entertaining no visitors. In the ten years I'd lived there I had yet to lay eyes on him. We shared a dense stand of cedars and impassable swamp, with only a strand of twisted barbed wire to mark the property line, strung straight through the middle of the bog.

The dear old bog.

I'd gotten my bright idea the first time I saw that brackish green stretch of no man's land, and had kept it in reserve while I worked on other projects, never dreaming at the start that I'd employ it anywhere other than in a novel or a short story. The bog was covered with a spongy layer of decayed vegetation, only inches thick, but resilient enough for a man to stand on if he was careful not to tear the fabric with the corner of a heel. How deep went the pool of muck and wriggler-infested water beneath it, I couldn't guess, but when I tested it by piercing the loam with an eight-foot pole of dead stripling, it never touched bottom, and slid out of sight when I let go of the end. Nor was there any way of telling its age. For all I knew, there were bones of woolly mammoths and saber-toothed tigers down there, still waiting to be exhumed after a couple of thousand centuries, on top of sixty million years' worth of dinosaur. There was no reason to believe that a newer and much smaller skeleton shouldn't remain there as long.

But I wasn't counting on even that. That was the beauty part.

It was a long walk from my house to the bog, much of it uphill. It was tempting to consider throwing Hufnagel into the back of the four-wheel truck in the garage, drive as far as the cedars, and carry him the last hundred yards to his final resting place. But that meant tire tracks, simplifying things for the boys from Homicide. I put on dark clothes against the chance of being spotted by a late-night hiker, hoisted my guest into a fireman's carry across my shoulders (he was stiff already, the strychnine having advanced the process of rigor mortis), and set out through the back door.

Forty-five wheezing, sweaty, mosquito-bitten minutes later, I came to the edge of the bog, which by moonlight glistened like fresh tar. The woods were alive with chattering raccoons, inquiring owls, and lead-footed squirrels, whose hopping gait through dry leaves sounded exactly like a SWAT team in full charge; I was shaking, and not just from fatigue. It's one thing to stand among sunshine-dappled trunks planning to dispose of a body, quite another to stand supporting the weight of that body in striped shadows squirming with nocturnal predators and one's own demons. I wanted to put Hufnagel down and rest. I didn't; what if he left a scent that might attract a cadaver-sniffing dog? I shifted the burden a little to relieve one set of screaming muscles and stepped onto the squishy surface of the bog.

For a panicky moment I wondered if that thin layer of long-dead flora would support my weight and Hufnagel's combined; I had a fleeting, vivid vision of the two of us plunging through icy, bottomless offal, my nose and throat and lungs choking with muck and algae, then blackness—Hufnagel and I joined for eternity along with all the other fossils.

But the surface held. Foul-smelling water bubbled up around the thick soles of my boots, forced through the porous moss and lichen and corrupted plant-flesh by my weight and Hufnagel's, but the loam didn't part. I took another tentative step, then another. It was like walking on a waterbed. I plunged ahead, growing more confident with each yard. I came to the wire that separated my property from Lundergaard's. I improved my grip on Hufnagel's arms and legs and high-stepped over it.

Trespassing.

With a murdered corpse, yet.

That was the big idea.

I wasn't arrogant enough to assume I was the only one capable of looking beyond the bog to its possibilities. Any homicide detective with enough head to keep his hat from settling on his shoulders would obtain a warrant to excavate that part of the property if he were sufficiently motivated by suspicion, find the elusive bottom, and drag it for a corpse.

But a warrant was only good as far as the strand of barbed wire. Beyond it was my neighbor's land, and without probable cause to suspect him of complicity (no danger there; no one could connect him with me, or for that matter anyone else), the police were barred from searching it. They probably wouldn't even consider it. Premeditated murderers are far too wary to bury the evidence on adjoining property. The risk of the neighbors selling out and the new owners developing the land and turning up the body with a power shovel was too great. Much better to dig the hole in one's own real estate and never move. A lifetime of self-imposed house arrest was a small price to pay to avoid discovery.

My case was different.

I had an accomplice.

His name was Uncle Sam.

The bog was registered with the county clerk as wetlands, and the Environmental Protection Agency in Washington prohibits draining and developing wetlands, which would endanger the wildlife that depends on the habitat. An act of Congress would be required to change the law, and since Congress acts about as swiftly as the brontosauri that dozed beneath my feet—and slower still considering the inevitable protest by the environmental lobby—I could have buried the corpse on my side, sold the property to a developer the next day, and gone to live wherever I pleased, secure in the knowledge that no bulldozer or backhoe would ever profane the bog's natural beauty and incidentally fork up Hufnagel. After all, I didn't own the property where he moldered, and no authority, local or federal, could unearth him.

Poor Hufnagel. The cokehead plagiarist never stood a chance against me and the District of Columbia.

For once in my life I'd kept my mouth shut about an idea. I'd been afraid I'd talk it to death and never write it. It occurred to me, as I trudged far enough onto Lundergaard's to prevent the remains from drifting back onto my side (and also to observe a reasonable margin of error on the part of the surveyors), that if I'd taken the same precaution elsewhere, Hufnagel would never have had the opportunity to take advantage of my trust and I wouldn't be forced to throw away a good plot situation on a real-life murder. But at least there was no one to educate the police. It would've been a joke on me if I'd told the little thief and there was an unfinished manuscript on his desk outlining my plans for his disposal, just waiting for the police to read.

Finally I stopped and lowered my burden to the ground; if the rippling sheet of compost I was standing on could be called that. I stretched, crackling my bones and lighting up all the pain points in my muscles, then took the garden trowel out of my hip pocket, squatted on my haunches, stuck the pointed end through the loam, and cut a slit three feet long. I dropped the trowel through the slit, having no more use for it, then slid Hufnagel by his collar to the edge, encountering no resistance at all from the smooth, moist surface of the bog. I got his feet in first; the rest was leverage. A little tip, and Hufnagel slid out of my life as quickly as the eight-foot pole I'd used to try to plumb the depth of his grave.

The job was finished. I'd thrown away the rest of the poison in a city Dumpster, keeping only the amount I'd needed to dispose of my pest problem, flushed the residue down the toilet, and washed the hand-mirror. The cheap bastard didn't own a car, preferring to ride a bus to the nearest crossroads and walk the rest of the way.

I thoroughly enjoyed the stroll back to the house. It was a mild night. I had no corpse to weigh me down and the squirrels no longer frightened me. They were just rodents, after all. A bit of strychnine, and poof! No more squirrels. That gave me an idea for a story. I had Hufnagel to thank for it, which balanced things out and filled me with happy remembrances of our friendship.

The detective's name was Congreave.

He was a sergeant, and from the dirty gray in his shabby comb-over and broken blood vessels in his cheeks, that would be his rank when he retired. He showed me his badge and I sat him on the sofa where Hufnagel had tooted his last toot and told me that Mr. Hufnagel had been missing for two weeks. An acquaintance had heard the missing party mention an appointment to visit me on the twenty-eighth, which if true made me the last person who had had any contact with him before he vanished. I said it was true, we'd had a drink or two and some enjoyable conversation, but I couldn't have been the last person to see him because we'd parted early in the evening so he could catch the last bus home.

"He missed it," Congreave said. "At least, the driver doesn't remember him boarding, and he knew Mr. Hufnagel well enough to talk to. He was a frequent passenger."

"Yes, old Huf was high on public transportation." I kept my face straight.

The sergeant's eyes got a little less dull. "Don't you mean he *is?*"

I smiled.

"Did I say 'was'? I must've caught it from you. You referred to him in the past tense."

He grunted. "Did he say anything about going away somewhere? He missed an important meeting with his publisher. Something about writing a movie tie-in."

Same old Hufnagel. Handed the chance to put his name on someone else's plot, he was inspiration itself.

I said he hadn't mentioned taking any trips. Congreave asked many more questions, wrote my answers in a grubby little notebook with a well-nibbled stump of pencil, thanked me for my time, and left.

Three days later he was back, more animated this time. He'd spoken with some people who remembered my grudge against the missing man. I told him that was water under the bridge, but he asked me if I'd consent to a search of my house and property. I refused indignantly. I'd given that inevitable question a lot of thought and decided that being too cooperative was as bad as obstructing justice, at least from a detective's suspicious point of view. He said that was my privilege and he'd be back.

He got me out of bed the next day at dawn, with a squad of officers, crime scene investigators, officious-looking dogs, and a paper covered with archaic printing, signed by a judge. They went through the house from the attic to the basement, then went out to join the team that was probing around the bushes looking for freshly turned soil. Late in the afternoon the backhoe arrived. An officer stayed behind to keep an eye on me while the rest gathered around the excavation site. I gave Congreave credit for recognizing the bog's potential much earlier than I'd predicted, based on the impression he made. I offered to put on a pot of coffee, but the officer declined. I put it on anyway. The sergeant might appreciate it when he came back empty-handed.

But there was no disappointment on his face when he showed up just before dusk. His eyes were bright and he was smiling. "You can change your story any time you like," he said. "I'd pick now. It could be the difference between twenty years and life."

I felt weak suddenly and started to sit down, but the sofa reminded me how clever I'd been, warned me not to fall for any tricks. I remained standing. Something made a purring noise and Congreave pulled a cell phone out of his inside breast pocket. He listened, then said, "Human, I'm sure of it. When? 'Kay." He beeped off, looked at me. "What'd you use, some kind of acid?"

"What?"

"Doesn't matter. Medical examiner's on his way. He'll know what you used to strip the meat off that corpse."

"Meat?" Some writer. My vocabulary had been reduced to single-syllable words.

"I guess I should be grateful," he said. "Bones are a lot less messy than your average eighteen-day-old corpse."

That confused me. In my mind I'd rehearsed every conceivable method of interrogation, and this one hadn't figured. I wondered if the bog contained some kind of scavenger that picked skeletons clean of flesh, and in doing so had dragged the remains back across the property line. Maybe the police had cheated, extended the excavation onto Lundergaard's. That was infuriating. Didn't we all have to obey the law?

Two hours later, we were joined by a scrawny middle-aged character, bespectacled and bald, dressed incongruously in a wrinkled tweed suit and rubber hip boots. He took off his glasses and rubbed his eyes. "Damn arc lights are going to give me cataracts. What's your victim's name?"

"Harvey Hufnagel," Congreave said.

"Well, unless her father wanted a boy, this isn't her."

"Her?"

"Remains are female."

"No mistake?"

"Pelvises don't lie."

Congreave scowled at me. "What are you, a mass murderer? How many more you got buried back there?"

I kept my mouth shut. I wasn't sure English would come out.

"You might want to stop talking before you give this gentleman grounds for a slander suit," the medical examiner said.

"You saying she died of natural causes?"

"No, I'm pretty sure that hole in her skull came from a bullet. But this gentleman couldn't have been five years old when it happened. Those bones haven't had skin on them in thirty or forty years."

"Bullshit."

"Cross my aorta."

"I've lived here ten years," I said. "I spent my whole life before that in Seattle."

Very soon I was alone. The medical examiner at least was polite enough to say good night.

But the sergeant wasn't entirely without manners. Two days later he knocked at my door and asked if he could come in. I was still sufficiently rattled from our last meeting to feel cold dread when I saw his face, but that evaporated when we sat down and he began to speak.

"I've made my share of mistakes, but when I'm wrong, I say it," he said. "You know your neighbor, Mr. Lundergaard?"

"I know of him. We haven't met."

"No surprise. He's a real hermit. He's going to be tough to crack, because he's been alone so long he's gotten out of the habit of talking to anyone except himself. But he'll crack. Those bones we found on your property used to be Mrs. Lundergaard. Her dentist is retired, but he still had her records, so the ID's positive. She and her husband had an argument, apparently. He shot her and threw her in the bog. Told everyone she'd left him. He came over on your side to dump the body so a search warrant at his address wouldn't turn her up. Pretty clever for an old Dutchman."

*Clever for anyone*, I thought testily; it appeared I was as guilty of plagiarism as Hufnagel, albeit unintentionally. But I was feeling charitable toward Congreave, so I kept the edge out of my voice. "What about Hufnagel?"

"Still open. FBI's tracking a serial killer who picks up pedestrians on country roads, cuts their throats, and ditches them at industrial sites. They think he came through Michigan last month. Maybe your friend ran into him on his way to the bus stop from here. Bad luck."

"Rotten." I shook my head sadly. I wanted to do a somersault.

He rose. "Anyway, sorry we gave you a hard time. We've got to be thorough."

"I understand. It's the same in my work."

"I almost forgot you're a writer. Not much of a story in Lundergaard, I'm afraid. He's sewed up tight, once we find the gun he used. He didn't dump it with his wife, so we're getting a warrant to search the bog on his side of the line. I'll be surprised if we don't turn up something useful."

# Now We Are Seven

*Don't be taken in by the western setting; this is emphatically a suspense story. When I was invited to contribute a story to an anthology called* Ghost Towns, *I asked myself a question: "Who says you can't scare the pants off someone in scorching daylight?"*

"Well, Syke, it appears to me you can't stay away from bars of any kind."

It was the first friendly voice I'd heard since before the bottles broke. I sprang up from my cot—hang the hoofbeats pounding in my skull—and leaned against the door of my cage. "Roper, you're a beautiful sight. Come to bust me out?"

"Why do it the hard way? Gold's cheap." He grinned at me in the light leaking from a lamp outside the door to the cells. Same old Roper, gaunter than the last time we rode together and kind of pale, but maybe he'd been locked up too. There was lather on his range clothes and his old hat and worn boots looked as if they'd take skin with them when he pulled them off. He'd been riding hard.

"If gold was cheap, I wouldn't be in this tight," I said. "I got into a disagreement with a local punk shell a couple hours ago, and now I'm in here till I pay for smashing up a saloon. I drunk up all the cash I had. I should of just went on riding through."

He sent a look over his shoulder, then pushed his smudgy-whiskered face close to the bars and lowered his voice. His breath was foul with something worse than whiskey, like the way a buzzard stinks when it's hot. "I'll stake you, if you'll come in with me on a thing. There's money in it and some risk."

"Stagecoach or bank? I quit trains. They're getting faster all the time and horses ain't."

"Bank, and a fat one. Look." He glanced around again, then drew a leather poke from a pocket and spilled gold coins into his other palm. They caught the light like a gambler's front teeth just before he pushed them back out of sight.

"Damn, you hit it already."

"I scooped 'em out of a sack they was using for a doorstop. They've got careless. It's been years since anyone tried to stick up the place."

"Bull. What stopped you from picking up the sack?"

"I didn't want to put them on their guard. I intend to go back with help and clean the place out. A sack of coins only goes so far, but what's in the safe could shore up the likes of me and you for life."

"If it's as easy as that, how come it ain't been stuck up in so long?"

"The local law's got a reputation. Fellow name of Red pinned on the marshal's star a good while back and shot five good men as they come out the door with the gold. Another man wanted in Texas and Louisiana tried to beat him to leather when Red braced him; he had the edge on everyone in New Orleans and San Antonio, including two Rangers, but Red put him in the ground with one shot. Things kind've fell off after that. I said there was risk," he added.

"Red who? A man with that behind him ought to have his last name plastered over six territories."

"Well, it's a sleepy little town name of Sangre, most of a day's ride from this jerkwater. Three hundred years back it was a mission. Some tin-hats from Spain used it to coin the gold they stole from the injuns down in Mexico and store it till they got back, only they never did. The folks that still live there each claim an equal part."

"No job's that good," I said. "Dry-gulch this Red and just ride out rich as J.P. Morgan? You're drunk."

"Ain't had a drop. I rode all night hoping to find a man experienced enough to help me get the bulge on that lawman. When they told me at the saloon you was in here I figured God must want me to be rich."

I drummed my fingers on the bars. "Well, I got a heap of doubts, but anywhere's better than here. First thing in the morning—"

"What's wrong with right now?"

"Court ain't open at night. You can't just settle up my bill with the deputy."

He was still holding the poke. He bounced it up and down on his palm, making the coins inside shift around with a pretty little noise. "I didn't hear him squawk when I slipped him one of these to let me in past visiting hours."

"I'd as lief not take the chance. If he gets a sudden fit of honesty, I'll have a cellmate."

"I'll just go and feel him out. I'm a fair horse trader, don't forget." He left before I could stop him, closing the door behind him and leaving me in darkness.

In a few minutes a crack of light showed and he came back in, rattling the key on its big brass ring in his hand. "Told you he was reasonable," he said, inserting it in the lock.

The office was dim, lit only by the lamp on the desk with its sooty chimney. The deputy sat on the edge of the light resting his head on his arms folded on the blotter. A bottle of busthead whiskey stood nearly empty at his elbow. He'd stunk of it when he locked me up. You just can't get good help in public service out on the frontier.

He was a sound sleeper. He didn't stir when Roper hung the key back on its peg and took down another to get my pistol rig out of a drawer in the gun rack. My hat was on the halltree, my bedroll leaned up in a corner, and I got those. We let ourselves out of the quietest room I've ever been in with a drunk passed out in it. He didn't snore so much as a Sister of Mercy.

My tough little piebald was saddled and tethered next to a big gray with Roper's outfit on it at a rail behind the jail.

"I got your horse and gear out of the livery after I left the saloon," he said. "I was pretty sure you'd take me up on my proposition."

I strapped my roll behind the cantle and stepped into leather. "I hope to hell you're right about that gold. I'm already into you for more than I'm worth."

He grinned at me in the moonlight, gathering his reins. His eyes looked as bright as if he'd had a stiff snort. I figured he'd helped himself from the deputy's bottle. "We'll work out something."

It was desert country. The sun came up red as a boil and made its way clear across the sky and we didn't meet anyone on the road. By daylight Roper looked even paler and more gaunt than he had at night; at times I swore I could see right through him, but that was the heat. It looked to be taking more out of him than it did me, though I never once saw him drink from his canteen, even when he poured some in his hands to water his horse. I was sure he had and I'd just happened to be looking at all that fine scenery—mesquite, cactus, and the odd darting lizard—but when I drank my last drop and he offered me his, it was almost full.

"This trooper I talked to one time said he'd been a camel-wrangler, some kind of cavalry experiment that didn't pan out," I said, corking it up and handing it back. "He said the critters can go a week without water. I didn't put any store in it then, but I reckon now you must be part camel."

He grinned, teeth long and yellow in his fleshless face, and slung the canteen back onto his saddle horn. "I don't seem to need as much as I used to."

Shadows were getting long when we topped a low rise and there was this little mud pueblo at our feet. It looked like some you see out in that waste, a cluster of rounded buildings, some caved in, around a well that didn't look as if it would give up anything but a bucket of dust. When Roper picked up his pace I figured we were stopping there to rest our horses in the shade, but then we passed a board from an old wagon nailed to a post with SANGRE painted on it in dusty brown letters that must have been bright red when they were new. My heart dropped straight into my boots at the sight of it.

"Hell, it's a ghost town. Why'd you want to pull my leg with all that gold talk?"

"Keep your spurs on, cowboy. How long you think it'd stay put if the place looked prosperous?"

I didn't say anything. I was biting mad. I was grateful to him for getting me out of a hole, but this dried-up pimple of a place didn't look like much of an improvement. If there was any water at all in that well I'd fill up my canteen and ride on to a town with life in it. That's how far my hopes had shrunk in eighteen hours, from a new horse and outfit and a spread of my own to just a wet whistle.

Sangre didn't look any more promising from the middle of it than it had from on top of the hill. The saloon was still standing with the roof posts sticking out in a row and no door, but the livery and general store had fallen in and I only knew the purpose of these establishments from their signs, painted right on the crumbling adobe in the same faded brown as the name of the town. I considered it an indication of ill fortune that the one building that looked sturdy enough to stand on its own happened to be the jail.

"I hope that marshal you told me about is one of your stretchers," I said, drawing rein. "If he ain't, he's the only other thing breathing in this bump in the desert."

"Oh, Red's real enough. The breathing part's up to you and me to fix."

I stepped down and tied up in front of the saloon without a word. I knew for sure then he was full of sheep dip, talking about bushwhacking right out there in the open where anyone could hear. That sickly look made sense now; he'd eaten a mess of crazy grass or drunk from a bottle of Dr. Sloan's thinking it was Old Pepper and it had cooked what little brains he'd had. I unslung my canteen and strode over to the well, ringed with rocks in the center of what had been the town square.

I couldn't see to the bottom, but it didn't even smell like water. The length of stiff rawhide that hung over the edge and down inside wasn't encouraging either; it looked brittle as hell and if there was a bucket on the end of it the bucket wouldn't hold so much as its breath. I started hauling anyway. I didn't expect to draw anything but desert.

There was weight on the end. That gave me hope, but not much. Sand's as heavy as water. I pulled up twenty feet of rope if I pulled up an inch, took hold of a wooden-stave bucket by its bail, stood it up on the edge of the well, and looked inside. When I saw what it contained I yelled and let go. The bucket fell to the ground and split open, spilling out a pile of bones.

It wasn't as bad as I'd thought at first. At second look they weren't human. I recognized a cannon bone and pieces of rib too big around even for Goliath and there were some thin hollow shards like pipestems that would belong to roadrunners or those little lizards that raced around on their hind legs like they had somewhere to go. I used the toe of my boot to separate a piece of oblong skull I figured belonged to a Gila.

Roper came over to see what I was kicking around. "Huh. Critters hereabouts must be as clumsy as fat acrobats."

"They couldn't've all fell in. Them horse bones wouldn't fit with the horse still attached. Somebody put 'em there."

"Kind of funny when you think about it."

"Kind of crawly. Who collects carcasses and dumps them in a well?"

"Injuns, most like. They do all that heathen stuff to keep their gods happy. Thirsty?"

"I'm dry as a deacon. You think I came here first thing to suck on some old bones? Where's your canteen?"

"I didn't mean water. Let's go in the saloon."

I stopped being grateful to him then. The jail back in town was starting to look good. "You fixing to stand me to three fingers of dirt? Who stocks a bar with nobody to sell whiskey to but horseflies and rattlers? Where's that bank stuffed full of double eagles? There ain't even a bank!"

"There's a bank, but there ain't no double eagles in it."

"I knew it, you—"

"I told you they're Spanish coins. They stamped them right here in town out of bullion they shipped in from Mexico." He took out his poke, plucked one from inside, and laid it on my palm.

It was about the size of a cartwheel dollar but heavier, with a foreign-looking jasper gaping off the edge and on the other side a ship. Even with the sun going down it glowered there in the desert like a small sun its ownself. The side with the head had Spanish writing stamped on it in a half-circle:

*MONTON DE HISPANIOLA NUEVA—*
*CIUDAD DE SANGRE*

"I'll be damned."

"Look at the date."

Roper was grinning that horse grin. "Now you want to take me up on them three fingers of dirt?"

"I'm buying." I flipped the coin high, caught it, and stuck it in my pocket. He shrugged and took the lead.

Inside, the saloon was as dark and cool as a cave. It didn't have any windows. It didn't have any bartender either, and only two customers. When my eyes caught up to the dim I saw the bar was a thick cedar plank laid across two barrels that might have been as old as that coin, and cedar shelves behind it holding up rows of squat bottles black as ink, with dust on them.

"Stock's limited." Roper stepped behind the bar as if he owned it. "What'll it be, wine or rum?"

"Wine, I reckon. I never had rum."

"When'd you ever have wine?"

"Rum, then. Where the hell is everybody?" I'd never seen a ghost town where a man could get drunk without bringing his own. Drifters would've cleaned the place out years and years ago.

"Siesta'd be my guess. Mex habits die hard in these here mission towns."

"I didn't see no mission. Anyway, siesta's always at noon."

"We passed it on the way in. Cross probably fell off the roof back when George Washington was a pup." Roper uncorked a bottle, sniffed at it, and thunked it down on the bar in front of me. Dust jumped up from the plank and settled back. "It was just like this when I rode in yesterday about this time. Place gets right lively come sundown. Everybody in town shows up."

"How many's that?"

"About five." He struck a match and lifted the chimney of a green brass lantern on a nail. What little light there had been was almost gone.

"Regular mee-tropolis, ain't it?"

"They're the five richest folks in the territory, don't forget. A fifth part of what's in the bank'd stake old man Vanderbilt to a bushel of railroads." He finished lighting the lantern and leaned his elbows on the bar. He hadn't gotten a bottle for himself. I asked him if he was keeping temperance.

"Ain't thirsty."

I didn't rise to that a second time. If he wanted to dry up and blow away it was his business; or perish from lack of sleep. If any piece of what he'd said was gospel he'd spent almost thirty-six hours in the saddle. The Roper I knew could snooze around the dial and still not run out of yawns.

I took a careful pull from the bottle. The place didn't seem to have glasses. The stuff inside tasted musty, but it had a nice little kick. I helped myself to a swig and started feeling better right away.

"What makes a rich man stick around a pile of buffalo chips like this?" I wanted to know. "I'd take my cut and light a shuck for Frisco."

"San Francisco's full of thieves," said a brand new voice. "Red can't protect 'em there."

I'd gotten so accustomed to just Roper for company I almost choked on rum. I spun around, scooping out my heavy Colt.

The woman I drew down on was pretty as daybreak, and about as scared of getting shot as a puff of warm air. She was delicate-boned, with a mass of yellow hair that fell in waves to bare white shoulders that looked polished. She had on a white dress with black spots and nothing holding it up but a pair of bosoms I could nearly see all of. Her feet were bare and she wore gold hoops in her ears like the women you sometimes saw dancing on tables down in Mexico, only she wasn't Mexican. She had blue eyes and red lips and little sharp teeth that showed when she smiled, as she was doing then. She stood in the doorway with one hand resting on the frame and the other on her hip.

"That there's Cora," Roper said. "Cora, meet Syke. He's skittish in the heat."

Sheepish was the word. I holstered the Colt and muttered a howdedoo.

She took me in without moving her eyes. They were the coolest things in that burnpatch, but they set me on fire worse than the rum. "Your friend looks healthier'n you, Roper. Been up to something you shouldn't?"

Now it was his turn to look sheepish. "Back off a dally, Cora. I'm a greenhorn."

"Green don't last out here. You best listen to good advice when Red's giving it."

I couldn't follow the conversation any more than a trail across rock, but I was starting to smell something bad and it wasn't the bones in the well. I turned on Roper. "You both sound tight with this here Red. I thought he was the lawman we're trying to avoid."

"It's a mite more complicated than that." He was looking at the ground now. That floor was made of dirt packed harder than iron.

Cora said, "Cork that jug, stranger. We got a business meeting to attend."

She stepped away from the door then. The pool of light from the lantern was lopsided and when she passed through shadow them blue eyes glowed like red sparks. I corked the jug. A little stimulant seemed to go a long way in Sangre. Anyway when she came back into the light her eyes looked normal, though not ordinary.

After that the place started to fill up, and nothing was ever normal again.

They slunk in without so much as a rustle of cloth or the clink of a spur—going out of their way, I thought, to avoid the shine of that lantern, like wolves circling a campfire. Three there was, ragged saddle tramps in greasy hats, shirts missing buttons, and Levi's faded white, with holes enough to embarrass a scarecrow. These clothes and their bandannas hung off skin and bone, and the shanks of their broken-down boots wobbled on their ankles so loose they could step right out of them if they lifted their feet high enough. As it was they shuffled, raising clouds of dust, and their eyes glowed red to a man, all but the one that was covered by a leather patch the man had cut right out of his vest, where it matched the hole. In a few seconds they and Cora and Roper had me half-surrounded in a piece of a circle like the writing on the coin in my pocket, with the bar at my back.

Roper was with them, I saw then. He'd stepped away and turned to face me with the rest. His eyes were alight too, but not as fierce, just a glimmer like the first weak spark from flint and steel. I hadn't noticed it last night, and we'd ridden miles in the dark.

I was shaking, but the weight of the Colt was back in my hand and settled it. None of them was packing that I could see.

"This the best you could rustle up, Roper? He don't bring much to the pot."

It was the man with the patch talking. I could smell his breath six feet off. It was worse than Roper's. It belonged down there in that well back when the meat was putrefying.

"I done the best I could with the time you gave me."

I turned my gun on Patch. "I got six slugs and there's five of you. Stand clear or I'll blow down the lot."

Roper said, "Put it up, Syke. It's a dogfall."

I swung the muzzle his way. "You just moved to the head of the line, you snake. All I got's my horse and outfit. You could've bought them fair and square for what you paid the deputy to bail me out instead of hauling me clear out here just to dry-gulch me."

"I didn't give him a cent. You didn't look at him too close."

"What'd you do, buffalo him? I didn't hear a shot."

Cora gave me a pitying look and turned on Roper. "That was taking a chance. You heard what Red said."

"I made it back, didn't I?"

The air changed, as if the saloon still had a door and someone had kicked it open, creating a current. The half-circle broke in the middle and someone tromped in to fill the space, raising more ruckus than the rest of them put together. He wore heavy silver spurs, the kind vaqueros wear below the border, and they jingled and clanked like irons on a condemned man. The boots they were strapped to were cavalry, the stovepipe kind with flaps that cover the knees, and they fit, but they were in as poor shape as the rest, run down and cracked. He had on a rusty black frock coat, cavalry trousers with stripes up the sides, with darns and patches, and a star on his lapel that looked as if it had been hammered out of brass by someone who didn't know much about smithing. A forage cap with a square visor sat atop a nest of hair that bushed out and tangled with a beard that covered him from cheek to brisket. It was the color of copper.

"I'll ante up and reckon you're the one they call Red." My voice was shaky but I reined it tight. I shifted my aim to him. He had six inches on the next tallest man there and more gristle than the rest combined and was the easiest to hit.

His eyes barely lit on me before shifting to Roper. They were coal black with no red in them, at least not there in the light.

"You fed." His voice was rainbarrel deep and hard.

"I had to." Now, *there* was a quaver for you. "It was a long ride into town."

"And a long ride back. For you, almost an eternity. I told you what happens after the first time. The sun won't hurt you until then. The effect may be delayed but not avoided. An hour this way or that can make a difference, and you wouldn't have survived a second dawn. You put us all at risk."

"He came through, Red." Cora sounded timid. I hadn't known her three minutes, but it seemed out of character.

"Don't take his part unless you want to have horse instead."

That silenced her. Red didn't yell, but his words rang like a hammer on an anvil. He seemed to have some kind of accent— Mexican, maybe, despite hair color and pallor—but it might just have been his careful way with the language I noticed, as if he was borrowing it and wanted to give it back just as he found it.

I cracked back the hammer. The Colt was a double-action but I wanted his attention.

"I come here for gold," I said, "but I'll just take my horse and go. Nobody's eating it tonight or any other."

The big man looked at me full on for the first time. "It wasn't your horse I was talking about. Roper's has served his purpose. Do you want to see the gold?"

"I seen it. I figure what I seen is all of it. If I wasn't hung over I never would've fell for no bank out in the middle of nowhere begging to be robbed."

"Hernando."

He barked the name without taking his eyes off me. A man with two little triangles of black moustache at the corners of his wide mouth turned and shuffled out. He was back in a couple of minutes dragging an army footlocker. At Red's direction he scraped it into the middle of the room and lifted the lid. It was filled to the top with yellow fire. The coins matched the one Roper had given me. The sight pretty near disarmed me, but I tightened my grip on the pistol.

"Go ahead, fill your pockets," Red said. "You'll need an explanation for how they came into your possession, but I've found gold has a way of evaporating suspicion. It makes partners out of strangers and friends out of enemies."

"Talk sensible. Roper said your job was to protect it from road agents."

"Admirable. Inspired, no doubt, by this star I made from a coin. The appearance of authority quiets newcomers long enough to hear my proposition."

"I knew you wasn't no law."

"But I am. Hundreds of men and women were slaughtered on my word alone, many years ago. Pardon my ill manners. Out in this waste one comes to neglect the proprieties. I am General Alejandro Rojas, late in the service of Charles, King of Spain and Emperor of the Holy Roman Empire. That's his likeness." He gestured toward the coins.

I laughed high and harsh. "You fried your brains in the heat. Them coins are three hundred years old."

"Three hundred thirty-three. I had the pressing equipment shipped from Gibraltar in 1537 and supervised the first run. Of course, that was before the curse."

I let him jabber. I couldn't get my mind off that footlocker. I'd raised my goal to include survival *and* making away with all it contained. I'd bluffed folks less simple.

"We drafted native labor to transport the gold from Tenochtitlan," he said. "We weren't subtle about it, and many of our prospects resented the whip and thumbscrew. One was a priest, who when we dragged him from the pagan temple said something in his savage tongue and spat in my face. Naturally I had him dismembered. I did not learn the significance of his action until the Hunger."

That distracted me from the gold. I remembered I hadn't had a bite in twenty-four hours. That rum on an empty stomach had commenced to make me hear things he couldn't be saying.

"*Chupador de sangre.*" He seemed to enjoy the taste of the foreign words; which weren't foreign to him. "Bloodsucker; a fresh title for my string. I was voracious, but the sight of solid food sickened me. Upon impulse I preyed on an Aztec slave. I was fortunate in that our expedition was only hours from home. I felt the weakness in the sun that Roper knows so well. I slept, satiated, but when the orb rose the following morning the first shaft burned me where I lay on my pallet. I fled for the darkness of the mission, where I avoided immolation, but the burn would not heal. Later I had all the religious iconography stripped away and buried. Once the building was desanctified I recovered. I am, as I said, cursed."

I kept my mouth shut. He was loco sure enough. I hoped he wasn't so far gone he'd try to jump an armed man. I'd drop him, but if the others joined in I'd have a fight on my hands.

He seemed to know what I was thinking. "Gentlemen. Lady."

The men wore bandannas around their necks, all except Red, whose throat was bare. Now they drew them down and advanced into the light. Each had two tiny craters three or four inches below the left ear, as if they'd tangled with barbed wire. Cora's showed when she swept back her mass of shoulder-length hair. Roper's looked redder and rawer than the others.

"I alone am unmarked," confirmed Red. "My condition was caused by black magic, not by having been fed upon. I am like Adam, who alone among men has no navel.

"We subsist on blood. When humans are unavailable—a chronic condition here—we make do with stray horses and other creatures that are barely sensate and so have no souls to animate them when they perish. Their remains go into the well, as the spectacle of a pile of bones might frighten away the intelligent bipeds we prefer. Do you know now why you've been summoned?"

I was feeling as pale as the rest, but I kept my grip tight on the Colt. "You got particular bedbugs is all; they favor necks. Now go fetch some sacks and get to work emptying that there box. I'm fixing to ride out of this crazy house a rich thief."

Roper said, "You always was slow, Syke. When you ride out, it'll be to fetch someone back to take the taste of horse and Gila out of our mouths. All the towns close enough to ride to and back are too far away for them that's fed to make it home before we burn up like ants in a skillet. I took my turn; now it's yours."

"Don't forget them coins for bait." This was the man with the patch on one eye. "See can you interest more than one in our little old bank. We'll be hungry an hour after you're sucked dry, scrawny fella like you. Roper's horse won't hold us nor yours neither, once you got your use out of it."

I laughed again, making out like I was enjoying myself. Truth was they had me jumpy as beans in Chihuahua, and half believing what they said there in the night. Come sunup I'd be laughing for real, by which time I'd be well on my way back to civilization, rich as Pharaoh. In another minute Red would be claiming him as a personal acquaintance.

"So you're all desperadoes," I said, "stuck in a trap set with money. What's that make Cora, one of them bandit queens you read about in dime novels?"

"She came with Perkins there, fleecing their way across the West with cards and the old badger game." Red indicated the last member of the party, with big ears and what must've been a honey of a pair of handlebars before the wax run out. "She was a windfall; although keeping her in clothes is a challenge. Some of our citizens come with changes in their bedrolls, but she's our only woman. Fortunately she's handy with a needle and thread. What she's wearing used to be a nightshirt."

"You like it?" She spun around on a bare foot, letting the dress billow. "I made the spots with dye from a deck of cards. I'm partial to patterns."

Red said, "Look for yard goods while you're about it. Cora let out these rag-bag items Patch brought back, but they want mending again. Think of it as a trip to town for supplies—and provisions."

"That's a right smart ghost story, but it's smoke. What keeps 'em from just riding on?"

The big man smiled, the teeth in the red beard as long as Roper's and as sharp as Cora's. "We would be more than six if that did not occur from time to time. Not much news reaches us, but I assume some got caught in the sun after they fed and then returned to the earth as dust. I can't imagine even a few others surviving long once townspeople started dying and coming back as one of us. There is always a wise padre or an immigrant from a European village versed in the old methods of destruction.

"It is not as tragic as you think," he continued. "You will exist without fear of age, illness, or death, and we are an entertaining crowd. I can tell you stories of the conquest, and Hernando knows all the gossip from the old Spanish court; he was a viceroy as well as a colonel under my command. He was also my first companion in this condition, after the Aztec slave I fed on passed the seed to him, then fled into the desert, roasting himself to a crisp. All the other soldiers deserted, which was a pity. What a mighty band of immortals they would have made!"

"Don't forget you're rolling in gold." Patch's sneer climbed one side of his face to his ruined eye.

"Quite right. You will have an equal share, and you can amuse yourself betting at cards or throwing coins at Cora's feet when she performs. She knows all the songs that were popular in St. Louis before she came to us thirty years ago."

"Red, you charmer," she said.

I'd had my fill of his charm. I shot him point blank.

When the smoke cleared he was still grinning. "That takes me back. You can have no concept of the relief I felt when a frightened corporal fired his matchlock in my face. Spanish armor was not designed for this climate. I let him run away with the others and took off the breastplate for good."

I fired again, with the same result, and tried my luck with the rest of the chambers. Roper was the only one rattled, but when he checked for holes and come up dry he blew a stinking blast of air my way and uncovered his horse choppers, which had grown pointy since the last time.

I stumbled back against the bar, knocking over the bottle of rum and fumbling at my belt for fresh cartridges.

Red seemed to lose patience. He pointed his shaggy chin at the one called Hernando, who lunged and seized my gun arm with cast-iron fingers. It went numb and the pistol thumped the ground. Roper got me on the other side, and although his grip wasn't nothing next to the foreigner's it was stronger than I remembered from arm-wrestling him. Patch and Perkins squatted and grabbed my ankles. I was pinned like a bug.

"Ladies first." Cora's face blurred as it came close, leaving only eyes red now in the light and those teeth.

I woke up in dead dog darkness and knew it was the mission where we all slept, though there were no sounds of breathing or any of the little stirrings that people make in their beds. They'd fed and were resting contentedly. I lay on straw scattered on hard earth.

They built those adobes to last in the old days—Red's time—with walls two feet thick and not a window or even a chink to let in light and heat, but I knew it was daytime just the same; I could track the sun across the sky by the throbbing in the holes in my neck. In a little while it would let up and I'd have the strength to sit a saddle. I hoped I could hold out longer than Roper without feeding, but I hadn't had anything but rum in so long I knew what it was like to be a gaunt wolf when game's scarce. I didn't want to make a mistake and burn up, and I didn't want to let anybody down. It was my turn.

# About the Author

An authority on both criminal history and the American West, Loren D. Estleman has been called the most critically acclaimed author of his generation. He has been nominated for the National Book Award and the Mystery Writers of America's Edgar Allan Poe Award.

E

MAY 1 0 2016